UNIVERSAL DEFENDER
<BOOK 2>

I0601999

FIRE TO BURN THE STARS

BY GREGOR FJELLREV

BLUE FORGE PRESS
Port Orchard, Washington

Universal Defender: Fire to Burn the Stars (Book 2)
Copyright 2021, 2022
by Gregor Fjellrev

First eBook Edition April 2021
First Print Edition April 2021
Second eBook Edition February 2022
Second Print Edition February 2022

ISBN 978-1-59092-948-3

Cover design by Brianne DiMarco

Blue Forge Press is the print division of the volunteer-run, federal 501(c)3 nonprofit company, Blue Forge Group, founded in 1989 and dedicated to bringing light to the shadows and voice to the silence. We strive to empower storytellers across all walks of life with our four divisions: Blue Forge Press, Blue Forge Films, Blue Forge Gaming, and Blue Forge Records. Find out more at www.BlueForgeGroup.org

Blue Forge Press
7419 Ebbert Drive Southeast
Port Orchard, Washington 98367
blueforgepress@gmail.com
360-550-2071 ph.txt

Crack your knuckles, Miles.
It's showtime, and they will all behold your power.

MORE BY GREGOR FJELLREV

Universal Defender

Book 1: Today I Save Myself

Book 2: Fire to Burn the Stars

Book 3: Enter Unmaker

Blue Flash

Miles Radien and the Cult of the Chaosmaker
(Universal Defender)

Veralis Stratenheim and the Bridge Across Fire
(Universal Defender)

Reticent (Angels of Anarchy)

Talenostrum

Night of the Whapwolf

In Combat with Time

www.BlueForgePress.com

UNIVERSAL DEFENDER
\<BOOK 2\>

FIRE TO BURN THE STARS

BY GREGOR FJELLREV

ACT I
RECLAMATION FROM HELL

Miles had tasted victory before, no doubt. His duel with Avanchenvaldr, the battle on Hulae, even what he did on Earth running the Fourteen Werewolves. But destroying the Opponent Unbeatable... that was the first true victory he could declare. A nightmare that plagued him his whole life, now forever defeated. That felt good, and it was the first time Miles had ever said that for what he could remember.

After a day in the city of Independence to 'debrief' himself, as it were, he spent the evening at Bringer's hole-in-the-wall tavern. It was only ever him and maybe two or three others, usually Ascendant, but that was the beauty of the place. It wasn't even that large in the seating area and counter, maybe only about the size of the average kitchen and dining room. But it didn't need to be any bigger.

"You look... satisfied," Bringer told Miles as he

poured the first pint for the victor at the counter.

"A great weight was lifted from my shoulders today," Miles replied. "A haunt that has burdened me for too long has been utterly vanquished at last."

"Well, good on you for sure!" Bringer genuinely declared. Over the time the two had known each other, Bringer seemed to be more and more invested and hopeful of Miles conquering his trials, whatever they were. Thus, he was quite enthusiastic to hear that Miles had done something so monumental on a personal level. "I suppose it's not my place to dig, but I can see that you really have done something good for yourself, and that brings me joy to know."

As much as it had taken a bit, Miles no longer felt it odd for a mechanical being to talk about emotions. After all, that question had been settled long ago in the bloodiest war in the universe's history.

Returning home eventually, Miles sat at the table, and closed his eyes. Once he heard the harmony of silence, he opened them to see the image of who he'd be if he could be anyone: himself but stronger. The effigy of a better version of Miles Radien.

"It was about time, I think," Miles said to the silent aspect of wisdom and strength. "Not too soon, and especially not too late."

Miles batted an empty glass around between his

<GREGOR FJELLREV>

hands that until a few moments ago, was full of water.

"Now that I think about it, that thing definitely was beaten at the right time. Any sooner, and it would've come back at some point. Any later, and... well, it might not have happened at all. So absolutely destroyed... that is a victory I am proud to declare."

Miles snapped his fingers and the spark summoned a flaming blue orb of The Aura's power. Not really flames in the traditional sense, more like 'energetic radiation.' But they certainly behaved like flames around the orb Miles tossed between his hands instead of the glass he was using before. "It doesn't even feel odd anymore. If my calculations are right, I've had The Aura for about three years now. But I figure time isn't going to be too heavily tracked by me as I participate in the universe."

With a clenching of his fist, Miles snuffed out the orb. "Veralis has been teaching me a lot. Even with what I've figured out myself, she's been a hell of a help with refining it. Sharpening it, and also making it less of a strain on myself to do these sorts of things. I actually recently figured out how to do this thing she called 'autotelekinetic cantrips,' these sort of Psionic sub-routines that I can program myself to inherently be able to do to make life a little easier. Sort of an 'everyday power' thing. Summoning small platforms just above the ground so that I don't sink up to my shins in mud or trip over roots and bushes, being able to quickly put my sword back in its sheath instead of doing that little 'sheathing dance' that sometimes happens... that sort of thing."

He paused for a moment. "Eh, if you know what I mean, you know what I mean."

Another silent moment passed. "For the first time in my life, I'm looking forward to where it might go next."

Miles then heard a knock on his door, and dismissed the Effigy. It was Veralis.

"Need something?" Miles asked.

"Uh... not right now, I don't think." Veralis responded. "Xenidar wanted me to let you know that the Humans have been recognized by the Conclave of Sentience, but declined being part of the actual Conclave itself, choosing instead to..."

Veralis grabbed the transcript from that very meeting she referred to.

"Quote, 'Operate independently as a species governing itself and its own needs, while also working alongside Turazin's Conclave of Sentience and their best practices to the best of... reasonability?' Okay, that last word is concerning."

"It's very human though," Miles said. "They're

<GREGOR FJELLREV>

basically saying that they want to be able to not listen to what the Conclave says without consequence. It's... it is very, very human."

"To me, this sets off an innumerable amount of red flags and alarm bells," Veralis continued.

"I'd be more concerned if it didn't," Miles affirmed. "The humans want to be able to say that they're either with or against the Conclave at a moment's notice, with zero accountability. The pursuit of deniability of commitment or responsibility to it is an extremely human trait."

"The Conclave did agree to the humans being on their own, and made it clear that certain protections would not exist for them as a result."

"That's kinda what the representatives are counting on, if you catch my meaning."

Veralis took a second, then managed to seem even more suspicious of the Human leadership's choices.

"Get used to that sort of behavior, as much as I hate to tell you," Miles finished.

Most of the rest of the day was in the Holographic Arena, something that Miles had almost become addicted to, to Veralis's curiosity.

"I mean, I can sorta get it, on a base level," she noted. "You've never seen technology like this before these days. But it seems a little more than that. Like you're... infatuated with the very concept of the Holographic Arena."

With a wooden Baston in hand, Miles parried the projected foe's strike, then smacked it twice on either side of the collarbone before kicking it down.

"I mean... you're not wrong," Miles said after catching his breath. "The raw fact that I can just... train. At-will. The fact that these projections are as intuitive and realistic as they are is just a bonus. But beyond that, I can just train whenever I want to. Whenever I want to. That's an idea totally alien to me, and it's still so surreal to just be able to say 'I wanna train right now' and then just be able to *do* that."

Veralis had a heavy look to her as she studied Miles with that. Like she understood everything he said, and even why, but just couldn't comprehend, let alone stand just what must have happened for him to get to that point.

"I remember I had a phrase back on Earth," Miles added. 'The sun will rise, the sun will set, and the Seattle skies will be grey.' A perfect purgatory is where I lived, and I don't think I'll ever stop being amazed by the raw ability to just *do* things. Especially if it's me who gets to do them."

"So what do you want to do now?" Veralis asked. "If you knew that at this exact moment, you could get any one thing you asked for, no matter how ridiculous or outlandish or even impossible, what would it be? A most primal of want, or longest-standing dream, or a place that provides it, and you knew in all ways all you had to do was say that you wanted it?"

"I... I can't think of that. As far as I understand, I've got it already. Maybe even just the knowledge of that is enough for me right now. I can't exactly say a vacation, because this *is* the vacation to me. This *is* everything already, having this house on Cynofrax, getting to hone my skills, travel across worlds, conquering challenges and putting those skills to the test. I mean, I'm already there as far as I'm concerned."

"Certainly sounds like it," Veralis said with a smirk.

Miles's comm-link and scanner pinged, so he grabbed it. The Redarian Jarrek Wöllschlager was contacting him.

"Jarrek. Good to see you, what do you need?"

"Can you be on Redaria Prime soon? I'd rather discuss in-person."

"Sounds good."

Jarrek was the first to hang up before Miles commented to Veralis, "Like I said, put those skills to the test. This is the dream I always had."

Miles had by this time, finished configuring the interior of the Aura Runner to his liking. The ship was

Archaeotech, built an absurdly long time ago with techniques and technologies, many still that can't be replicated, including reliable bigger-on-the-inside pocket dimensions in enclosed spaces like the Aura Runner's interior wings. As the ship traveled to Redaria Prime, it was just fine detail work. What foods and drinks were in the Sustenance Wing, what weapons he could train with from the Armory Wing, better organization of stuff in the Cargo Wing-

"This is New Klosaan Starport, requesting confirmation of identity and purpose of visit." The space equivalent of an air traffic controller transmitted. Miles quickly ran back to the cockpit to respond, as he had reached Redaria Prime while he had been working.

"This is Miles Radien in the Aura Runner, confirmation CN nine-twenty-six, visiting on request of Arch-Militant Wöllschlager, also leisure."

"All right, Aura Runner, you're clear to land on platform A-90. Welcome back, Radien."

"I've never been tired of coming, Viks."

Miles continued his course and landed on platform A-90, and walked over towards a nearby automated terminal to rent a vehicle. A Redarian he didn't recognize approached him, handing him a note.

"Is the clandestine stuff necessary?" Miles asked.

"The Arch-Militant seems to think so," she

replied. "Between you and me, he only does this when what he wants to attain information that would normally be against protocol or procedure, or whatever the word of the day is."

Miles looked over the typewritten note, reading a local address. "So it would seem. Who should I be thanking for the assist?"

"Micah Jorvask, Disciple of Shadow, 1st Degree."

Miles nodded, and Micah left, grabbing a device he hadn't noticed she put down, a signal jammer. Any recording devices that were in the area would've recorded nothing of their meeting. Miles soon acquired his transport, a distant cousin of the touring motorbike whose name was almost unpronounceable, that name being the 'Xnopyfth Speeder,' roughly pronounced 'hnopiffth.'

The address was for a house on the outskirts of the city itself, near Redaria Prime's Neutral Zone. Much like Sectora Neutros on Cynofrax, the non-province that made up a little over half of the habitable surface consisted of self-governed townships and communities that still gave their allegiance to the overall goals of the planet.

Miles knocked on the door to the house, and Jarrek answered.

"I forgot you wore glasses," Miles noted.

"Ocular HUD. Sometimes I can't trust my own eyes to tell me everything I need to know." To this, Miles nodded in agreement.

"D-o-S 1st Degree Jorvask got me here," Miles clarified next. "I remember that you prefer to hear who actually delivers messages."

"Aye, and Micah is someone I trust. Honestly, if this had to do with any other species than the Humans, I would've asked her. But if there's any Human I can trust, it's you."

"I appreciate that. Veralis already informed me of how they handled their recognition by the Conclave, and I share the concerns I'm sure many people have."

Jarrek brought up a holographic map of the second Human world, the one that the Conclave gave them. "They've called it Fortem Terra Nova, and its capitol has been designated as New Oslo."

Miles laughed at the name. "I cannot say I'm surprised, and I will now recommend a Human author by the name of Aldous Huxley. But what do you need from me?"

"Officially, nothing. As far as any records are concerned, we all eagerly await the accomplishments of a great and bountiful human empire. Off the books, however, I'll be blunt: I need you there as our spy for now. And when I say 'our,' I more mean 'the rest of the universes.' Any information you give me won't have your name anywhere near it. Anonymous tips from the occasional good samaritan, whatever cover might be needed. Redarians are well known for being able to smell trouble. And the Humans reek of it."

"I certainly don't disagree," Miles said. "Not all Humans, but enough of them for sure. I'll have to do it as I see fit, but I don't think that'll be too much of an issue, given that the kind of person I am is rather known both on Earth, and to others."

Jarrek nodded. "Once anything relevant is in my hands, I can make sure that it gets made known correctly. With no implications to you or our arrangement."

"As long as that remains the case, that sounds good. I suppose now is the time to head to the brave new world and check it out for myself."

Miles took the Aura Runner towards the new Human world. "Fortem Terra Nova... of course they would," he muttered to himself as he approached. It sure looked the part of a beautiful, ripe new planet for the Human race to ruin.

"Craft, please identify yourself," was the message that greeted him.

"This is Miles Radien piloting the Aura Runner, requesting entry to a Fortem Terra Nova Starport."

"Miles Radien... you're from Earth One, aren't you?"

"Aye. Ever hear of that Demon in Edinburgh? I killed the bastard."

"Ah. Well, the Devil of Edinburgh story is well-known, not so much the person who killed her. I'm transmitting the list of Starports that can take your craft at the moment, take your pick, I suppose."

Every single one of the cities was just the "New" prefix before a major city on Earth. New Oslo, the capitol, New Rabat, New Belgrade, even a New Tacoma and New Cahokia. Miles had always wished he could have visited the original. No New New York, though. He thought for sure he'd see that, and be able to joke about it endlessly.

"I'm just glad it's not New Seattle," Miles commented, selecting the closest thing to familiar territory to start in.

"Between you and I? Me too," the controller commented. Miles continued his course and landed in New Tacoma, which was ironic since this city was in the plains, not even near a river, let alone sound to build a port on.

There weren't any obvious landmarks that made this place clearly a New Tacoma, to which Miles was relieved, for one dominant reason, which he said to himself aloud.

"I'm really glad they didn't bring the Dome. Place had terrible acoustics."

"King Dome was worse, though," someone who heard him commented.

"Yeah, but they actually were smart enough to tear it down. One of the few things Seattle ever got right officially."

"So I'd guess you're originally from Eastern?"

"Actually, no, more peninsula. Not far enough in to be one of the peninsula hicks, but close enough to suffer the out of towners who thought the whole place was the Sound, and thankfully, far enough from Seattle that a pint wasn't the same price."

The both of them had a laugh before the Human introduced himself as Ellan Hector.

"I suppose we both digress, there's better things to do than have a measuring contest of old knowledge," Ellan stated, to which Miles nodded, and a decent pause in the conversation followed.

"I do always hate that butt-sniffing portion of getting to know someone. It feels so scripted and soulless," Miles said, and Ellan nodded this time. "But from the looks of things, the Conclave is making more sure nowadays to let the right ones in."

"As best they can. You hear about the bullshit our so-called 'reps' did on Turazin?"

Miles raised an eyebrow, even though he already knew the answer.

"I'd hoped we'd leave the wordy non-answers on Earth to rot with the people who talk them," Ellan finished with a sigh. "How even could we... integrate into how this all works? The people leaving Earth are getting first chances they never could've dreamed of, yet are so quick to forget how much they were getting kicked in the gut back there as soon as the smog clears."

Miles nodded solemnly. "It was all a crushing grey. But there's little sense, if any to reminisce about our misery, especially when we've got the capability at last to move forward, however that looks."

"I take solace in that not long after that animator turned out to be a literal Demon, there was a brief but potent anarchy across the planet. Most nation-states just stopped existing, and everyone went straight for the politicians and the rich fucks. The whole world agreed without saying a word, *none* of them can *ever* be allowed to leave the planet they wrecked."

"That was something I wasn't present for, given my hasty leave." It was at that moment Ellan recognized Miles as the man who killed Avanchenvaldr, and told all of Earth that it wasn't alone. "What happened to the people who were suddenly freed?"

"Overall? None of them are alive today. Whether

because people hunted them down, or they ate a bullet 'cause they couldn't live with what they'd done, or just died in the aftermath. It was almost surreal, though. Nobody even paused for them. Normally, when someone despicable dies, you've got the celebrants and the people shaming them because of self-righteousness, and the other shamers because they sided with the bastards. But... not those guys. Very few celebrated, but no one ever missed 'em."

Another pause.

"I mean... is there anything that needs doing around here, for lack of a better question to ask?" Miles asked, given the collective disdain for the typically scripted conversations that are usually used to get to know someone.

"Hmmm... for someone like you? I can't think of anything. But if this place, or just about any other city here holds true to their originals, I'm confident something will come up to suit you."

Miles soon found himself wandering around and eventually, outside the city of New Tacoma, past the residential suburbs that soon gave way to a great field of grass and scattered trees, a forest in the distance. Hours passed before he even realized as he wandered those plains, finding a strange bliss in it all.

"This is what I wanted to do, yeah," Miles finally

said to himself. "Wander the plains, monologuing dramatically to myself. Contemplating the things and making grand soliloquies on the musings of the nomad eternal. Hearing no voices of humans, no sounds of their contraptions. No roaring engines and blaring horns, no shouting of idiots, or the drone of buildings, being built, torn down, or used, or the planes overhead as the stone cherry on top of a bland, grey sundae. Wind makes noise, noise you can hear even among everything else. But there's a special kind of incredible when you're the only creature for dozens of miles. A strangely incredible noise when it's only the wind..."

He paused and listened to that noise.

"A noise I've never heard until this very moment."

Miles stood there for minutes, it was the first time he could recall it ever being that kind of quiet.

"Why the fuck did it take so long just to get something so simple?"

The contemplation was interrupted by a heavy tremor. Something just warped into the atmosphere of the planet. And it wasn't friendly. Miles turned around and saw in the sky a massive ship that looked like it was carved from a volcano. Grabbing his scanner and pointing it at the dark and red mass, he tried to figure out what that thing was, and the scanner told him something he really didn't want to see.

\<GREGOR FJELLREV\>

SCAN CONFIRM
DESIGNATION: DEMONIC BATTLE BARGE
ORIGIN: HELL

It seemed unreal to see that word on his scanner. Yes, it was from Hell, it was a Demon ship. So it obviously would be. But such high technology assigning a rather archaic name to where this thing came from was unnerving as it was factual.

Miles warped back to New Tacoma, which was in this ship's ominous shadow, and grabbed one of the persons fleeing towards their vehicle to leave the city.

"Where's the nearest military base?!" Miles ordered. The man simply pointed at the ship, and ran. No answers from this scared soul. Miles cursed and looked on his scanner for the local map, then found what he was looking for, and warped there.

"What the hell? Stop him!" someone from the base shouted upon seeing Miles, and several people grabbed guns to point at him.

"Sure, point a gun at me if it makes you feel better, but I'm here to help," Miles commented.

"Get him out of here, we can't have civilians interfering with the defense!"

"Chief, are you nuts?! Dude just appeared outta nowhere! If he wanted to fuck us up, he'd've fucked us right the hell up!"

The decision was made quicker than Miles thought it would, but there was just as much conflict in it as if it took ten minutes instead of ten seconds.

"Goddammit, fine. I guess if you can just hop in here like that, you can do more. Who are you, what can we do against *that?*" This man wasn't the base commander, but he was probably the closest thing to it in the room.

"Miles Radien; I killed the Devil of Edinburgh. Also took out a city's worth of Demons while Earth was getting its collective shit together. My guess is they're here to reclaim what was once theirs."

"The planet?"

"No, the species. The Dark Six once planned to use the Humans as their catalyst for invasion, and they don't like giving up what they call their property easily."

"We're not their property, no matter how many people served them before!"

"Then let's prove it!" Miles affirmed. "Has this planet got a Defense Grid? If you have, activate it now, and any surface to air automatic systems! It'll stop the majority of the craft from getting to the ground! There's only so many Demons on that Battle Barge!"

"Get to it!" the Lieutenant yelled, followed by several ayes from others as they powered up automatic planetary defenses. Admittedly, there weren't many, but there also weren't none. The Hajivakk had supplied a Planetary Defense Grid, though. So that was likely the most helpful thing of all.

"Right, with that breathing room, I can tell you some more you'll want to know," Miles explained. "That Battle Barge's very existence means that the Demons desperately want this planet, because that thing's had to sit in the void between galaxies for several billion years just to avoid detection. Meaning that we take that thing down, or at the very least make it easy for someone else, the Demons are fucked six ways to Sunday on Fire. Also, one of your boys on comms had better be getting ahold of some other species, they'll come sprinting to stop Demons. We're not far from the Glass Reflex system, home of the Ascendant. Send a message to Contrast, they won't hesitate to reinforce."

"We're hailing Contrast now, per instruction!" the communications officer yelled out.

"Also, Lieutenant, I need you and every man and woman in this base to get over the culture shock right now about the fact that the Ascendant are androids. They're sentient, and they've *been* sentient for longer than Humans have been around. The question of their sentience was answered 'yes' in the bloodiest war in the universe's history. So either accept that these guys have souls, or die mad about it."

"Warriors are warriors," the Lieutenant stated. "It's not me you need to worry about."

Miles nodded, and the Communications officer came to them with an update.

"Contrast is warping over seven... 'Galleon-Class Battlecruisers,' including their flagship, the Obsidian Spike."

"That means about fifty thousand crewmen and soldiers in ships twice the size of aircraft carriers. Demonic incursions aren't taken lightly. That means we need to hold the Demons here until the Ascendant arrive. Which... unfortunately means we need to make sure they don't have a reason to run away."

"What are you suggesting? It'd best not be to lower our shields."

"No, but weaken them. Or, feign it. Drop the shield's overall percentage power manually, but keep it online. Give 'em the appearance that they're breaking through. It'll have the added benefit of them having false information on how much punishment those Defense Grids can take. What's the ETA of the Ascendant reinforcements?"

"About ten minutes warp from here!"

"Ten minutes is all we need. Lower the power of the Defense Grid by seven percent each minute, but no more than ten! If you lose ten percent power over a

<GREGOR FJELLREV>

minute only give three on the next! We need to make it look natural, like they're actually about to get through! So the deactivation needs to be outside going in!"

"Defense grid dropping to ninety-six percent power."

"Sir, the Battle Barge is increasing its firing output!"

Miles was quick to reassure, "Keep the drop steady, funnel power into the inner layer of the shield as necessary! It'll look like we're trying to desperately bolster it."

"Gemini Missile batteries are now locked onto what we think is their fighter craft bay!"

Miles had another thought just then. "Note where it is, then move the lock a hundred meters wide before firing! Remember, we're just holding out until the reinforcements warp in, and we need to keep looking like we're worth it!"

The missile lock was adjusted, and the payload fired. After it impacted, the station started to receive a signal from the Battle Barge. The Demons were hailing the base, and Miles saw the opportunity to keep stalling them, so he told them to open the channel and be prepared for ugly. The screen turned on, and the Demon commanding the Battle Barge seemed a little surprised at Miles's presence.

"I suppose I expected this much disarray, but to see it when Avanchenvaldr's slayer led the Human defenders?" the Demon commander taunted.

"To whom do I speak, or will I have to call you a Nameless?" Miles fired back, to the Demon's rage as he spat fire on a nearby console from the insult.

"You are in a poor position to insult Darkstar Maaroth!"

"Everyone, listen carefully now," Miles said, glancing around, and momentarily fixing his eyes on the communications officer, who held up eight fingers out of frame, and Miles gave a very slight nod to acknowledge. "A little context, Demons earn their names. They have to do something very, very impressive and they are then named after whatever they were doing at the time. Maaroth, is a Demonic word for 'to hide.' Specifically, 'to hide from pursuers.'"

Maaroth screamed a curse at Miles that quite honestly, he was relieved to know that the Humans couldn't understand it.

"The barrage is getting more intense, sir!" one of the officers in the room noted. "Defense Grid at seventy percent!"

"Keep funneling like I said!" Miles reiterated. "Regardless, Maaroth. I can only assume you're here to take back what the Dark Six seem to be under the impression is theirs?"

"Your species dutifully performed their roles as pawns for the Old Lords! And the Lords will have their servants back!"

"Come and get them, then," Miles said, before signaling to kill the channel. Once that was done, he spoke again. "Yes, I wanted him pissed at me, it'll keep him persistent so that the Ascendant get more time to wail on him! At this point, he's stayed too long to warp out unscathed by the reinforcements, any more time he stays here is more Demons killed, and a higher chance of him getting his ship destroyed outright! Keep anti-air defenses locked on any surface-bound craft, I know we don't need to keep those off the Defense Grid, but this is a charade we're putting on, remember that!"

"I do have to ask, though, what did he mean by 'Darkstar?'" By this time, the base commander had entered the room, been briefed on the nature of Miles's assistance, and had heard the conversation just before.

"That's the type of Demon he is. Darkstars are the tacticians of Hell, and are second in rank only to the Dark Six themselves. Remember, though. This is an ancient ship, it's been lying in wait for orders since the end of the First War for Reality. So any Demon commanding it has all those billions of years worth of impatience and archaic arrogance."

The shield continued to hold, though overall dropping in its feigned failure. Tension in the room was high, and most communications were focused now on keeping mass panic out of the civilian equation, despite the fact they needed to not be aware that it was an act, this almost failure. Of course, there was a point to be made in that no one on the ground had ever seen a Planetary Defense Grid in action, so they wouldn't even know what it would look like if it was faltering. Finally, Miles heard the two words he had been waiting on.

"Reinforcements, sir!"

"Well, that went quicker than I thought it would."

The Ascendant Battlecruisers warped in at that moment, one of them accelerating forward and ramming the Demon capital ship with a pointed bow that made it the equivalent of a Space Trireme, and the cannon and laser fire tore the cursed floater to shreds. The debris of the ship harmlessly vaporized against the Defense Grid, which now comfortably recharged itself.

All of the Ascendant ships, save for the Obsidian Spike warped out, and the flagship stayed behind both to make sure the job was done, and to debrief the Humans below. A channel was opened between Miles and the Obsidian Spike's captain, Frame.

"Interesting diversion you employed, in that case," was Frame's comment after Miles explained exactly what his plan had been. "Admittedly, had that Battle Barge been under the impression it couldn't have won that fight, it would have fled. Then I suppose we'd be arguing about whether or not it was really there and that would lead to a frankly time-wasting phantom chase in the name of convincing the Conclave that the Humans can do things other than lie."

"I'm glad nobody's credibility had to be put at stake." Miles said, and the base Commander nodded. "Captain Frame, this is Commander Jonas Markusen, he's the one in charge of this base. I suggest further business regarding Fortem Terra Nova's defense be run by him."

"Very well," Frame acknowledged. He and Jonas soon came to the arrangement that an Ascendant cruiser would act as the first line of defense for Fortem Terra Nova, until the planet was able to launch a defense platform of its own. The Obsidian Spike, however, would not be the ship left behind, evinced by its warp-out to collect a different ship for the planet's immediate security.

"We're not a Conclave species," Jonas told Miles. "Hell, our reps basically told 'em that we wanted all the fun and none of the responsibility, and it's got everyone giving the Humans the stink eye. Why would the Ascendant help us anyway? Why would anyone at all?"

"Conclave or not, Demons threaten the whole

<FIRE TO BURN THE STARS>

universe," Miles replied. "And they certainly don't care whether you're specifically on the Conclave's side or just when it's convenient, 'cause the Demons will slaughter all the same. Naturally, it's within the best interests of the Conclave to not be massive hypocrites on the front of morality. Can you imagine the kind of image it would present, that the Conclave has more care about who's in it or not than the Demons?"

Jonas nodded. "Still a bit surprising, given our... troubled history."

"I too had to learn for the first time once, that the Humans aren't the only species in history to be a 'trouble' species. And I am still surprised that we're not the worst the Conclave has seen, outside of Demons."

A moment paused before Miles said something he realized that he hadn't said for some time.

"I'll have to ponder on that."

By ponder, it usually meant he spoke with the Effigy regarding the topic. But the phrase itself, he hadn't said it for quite some time. Not since he had been granted his power. Perhaps he'd have to ponder why that was the case as well.

Returning to his home on Cynofrax, Miles constructed a small area within the basement, hidden behind a false wall in the room with the Holographic Arena. A small room with a table, two earthenware cups, and a cabinet and fridge of various drinks that made for good pondering as they were consumed. This was usually fortified wine and mead. The fridge was stocked with caffeinated sodas, though. Just in case one didn't need the extra pondering-capable nature of harder drinks.

"Let's try it, then," Miles said as he sat down at one end of the table, and closed his eyes to summon the Effigy.

"Today has planted an interesting seed in my mind," Miles told the Effigy, who sat down across from him. "I knew the Ascendant would come. Regardless of what species was in danger immediately, if Demons are involved, all of creation is in danger. But even so, the apparent caution a lot of Humans are having regarding their own selves is only slightly reassuring. I think it's only as prevalent now because of the scrutiny that the Humans are under, and whatever process is going on in screening those who want to leave Earth. So what happens once that part is over, and the Humans are considered to have grown their cosmic sea legs?"

Miles wasn't sure if the Effigy was pondering this as well, but it sure looked like he was at least thinking about it.

"Something gnaws at me, something else, though," he continued. "I just know it, that somewhere down the line, there's something lying in wait to bring me the sobering reality. And not the worst kind of all, mind you. But rather, the one that tells me that Humans aren't the only evil race in the cosmos. I might know it on a factual level now, that 'of course the Humans aren't the only shitbags because that's literally impossible from the sample size,' but I've yet to see it firsthand. I haven't yet come across the time where someone, not a Human, does something that I could only think a Human would do…"

Miles downed the cup that was in front of him, just before remembering that he had put some Port in it.

"I fear that day will bring my darkest hour."

ACT II
THE OLDEST TRUTH

Miles dismissed the Effigy, and went to his workshop to draft out an idea he just had. Not for a techpiece, but something different.

"Autotelekinetic Cantrip Plan—Codename 'Equilibrium,'" he first wrote, before further notes on what exactly he needed to be enhancing within his body and mind with The Aura. It would require a considerable amount of meditation as his being altered itself to become capable of just what it was he wanted, not to mention just naming the enhancements he was to make, and making sure they were defined well enough to be doable.

Veralis entered the room. "You planning on using the Holographic Arena for a while, or should we run it together?"

"Uhh... I was not planning on using it for some time, but did you want to spar, or...?"

"Actually, I was gonna make it run an Encounter, wondered if you wanted in."

Miles nodded, and put the drafting paper down. For all their separate capabilities, he did have yet to actually test how he'd fare alongside Veralis in battle, as opposed to across.

"Load encounter, designation AT-99," Veralis instructed. The Holographic Arena then created a ruined suburb that acted as a battlefield. "Whoever kills the least makes dinner tonight." She then bolted off into the fray with her axes in hand.

"Wait, what?!" Miles shouted, but she was already gone into the thick of it, and Miles cursed mildly before conjuring the Borfblade and searching for Demons of his own to fight. The Arena's computer was taking a tally of how many each were killing on their own, and giving half a point to both if it was a cooperative kill. Miles went into one of the houses, and started his work there, slicing through the projected opponents, parrying and countering their attacks. From a window on the second floor, Miles saw Veralis kick a Demon onto a wrecked car, impaling it on the jagged ruin of the open door. Charging forward with a yell, Miles bashed his foe through the window, throwing it onto the street below, and dead. A few bolts to cut down the remaining combatants later, and Miles jumped from the window and onto the roof, before hopping off that and joining Veralis on the ground.

It continued for some time, this two versus all, throughout which both had 'stolen' kills from the other with cheeky knife throws and well-timed bolts of concentrated Aura energy. Soon, the streets were empty. But the simulation was still running, meaning there was still at least one they had missed. Miles scanned the battlefield using The Aura's Sight, and Veralis just waited for him to find the bugger for her.

She then blasted a house that Miles was staring quite intently at, thinking that the Demon was in there. In reality, Miles was watching the Demon's movement via peripheral vision, and took the chance of Veralis's distraction to blow up a nearby car the straggler was actually hiding behind.

But when the program terminated to reveal their scores, it turned out it didn't particularly matter who got the last kill. It was 44 to 51, Veralis's favor.

"I'm inclined to not count the first few of yours with that damn 'threetwoonego!' you pulled at the start," Miles remarked.

"Eh, fine," Veralis replied. "Even then, I've still got you beat by at least five."

Miles grumbled off towards the house's kitchen to prepare his Soup For The Darkness, enough for two.

"And it has to be something actually dinner-worthy, not just Soup For The Darkness!" Veralis's voice said from afar, to which Miles only responded with more intense grumbles. He was admittedly far better at making drinks than food. Even so, it had been some time since Miles had made the macaroni and cheese recipe that made the Fourteen Werewolves on Earth a sleeper hit among road trippers. And with some of the cheeses that Cynofrax had to offer, it made for somehow an even better version.

Even though Veralis could, like Miles, not need sleep, she often chose to anyway. Miles, however, preferred to take full advantage of the new time that not needing to rest created. But it was also the case he didn't want to disturb her while she did so, given their living together. During these nights, Miles would wander a forest near his home on Cynofrax. Relatively near, that is. It was actually ten miles away, but that distance was trivial with The Aura.

"It's not the same old woods, but it certainly feels like it," Miles said to the Effigy as they walked, referring to the woods near what home he had on Earth. "Normally one might expect the opposite to be the case, where it doesn't feel the same, but that trope is defied with Cynofrax's forests."

The Effigy, of course, just walked and listened.

"I should be over that damn planet by now," Miles continued. "I never have to go there again, and I hope I never will. I have what I've always wanted: my escape. I suppose there's something to be said about remembering where you came from, so that you appreciate this new life, but I still get the feeling that I shouldn't be on about it like an estranged ex-partner."

Miles then sat down on a tree stump.

"I never had one of those. Partners or ex otherwise. I don't call that a bad thing, though. I would rather never love at all than love and lose. I mean, that is what I've done... But losing at everything else tends to make one not care about victory as much as not being defeated. But I am glad that 'relationships' are not another defeat on the list."

The effigy sat on a nearby log a few feet across from Miles.

"It's the oldest truth of mine, a fact I have known since I could know fact. Radien stands alone. That's not bad, though. There is strength to be found in solitude, since no one can betray you if you're all that's there. As shit as my time on Earth was, I'm willing to say that it's given me the strengths I need to do what must be done, when those times arise."

Miles stared at the ground for a moment before turning back to talk to the one figure who always had been there.

"I can never let that fact become a bad thing. It's a fact all the same, whatever I think of it. Radien stands alone. I may as well turn it into my strength. Because when I say 'Radien stands alone,' the emphasis is not 'alone,' it's 'stands.' It's not a matter of 'despite all my standing, I am alone,' but instead a matter of 'despite that I am alone, I do still stand.'"

"Words of the fortress," a voice said from somewhere in the trees. Miles shot up from where he sat, dismissing the Effigy, who he could've sworn had stood up with similar urgency. "The tired fortress."

"Who dares?!" Miles shouted. "And how did I not know of your presence before?!"

A wisp of a dark green trail of fog flowed from one tree, then another, and several more before it coalesced into a form.

"Here is a form you can understand, if it helps," the spirit said, though on this body there was no mouth or eyes, but a vague shape of a forest spirit.

"Aye, spirit," Miles said, bowing his head slightly. "Now I get it. Did you have input, or do you just not get a lot of people you can talk to?"

"Both, I suppose." The spirit returned to a foggy form, then seemed to compress itself into a single point of leaf-green light before a few more points rose from the ground, and allowed the spirit to take a more corporeal form, the slightly more defined shape of a large, spectral bird. "You spoke to someone, though, when you said those words."

"A creation of my imagination," Miles clarified. "The person I can always talk to, who does not exist within reality. The one being I can't be a bother to."

"Yet now you talk to me as though I am that imaginary being."

"Because you approached me, wishing to speak. The Effigy is someone I can approach at will, and never fear being an inconvenience."

If a spectral bird could sigh, that was the sound the spirit just made. "I must say, in all my hundreds of thousands and millions of years, it has never gotten easier to see those like you."

"Then I will leave, I understand that to hear someone grouse is naught but tiring," Miles said, turning around before the spirit appeared in front of the path out and blocked his way.

"Not what I meant. But I assume you didn't want to take the chance, out of a want to not impose."

"Stole the words from my lips." Miles chuckled. "What would you have me do, though? What will you say that I haven't heard a thousand times from everyone else?"

41

"I will say that you will hear no run of the mill heartfelt speech about opening up from me."

Miles froze. "Well... that is correct. No one in my life has ever told me that. They always give the speech."

"I think you'll find that of those on Cynofrax, no one gives the speech. And do always feel free to wander these woods again, just in case you weren't sure."

The spirit then dissipated, and left Miles to his own devices, the first action of which was to summon the Effigy again.

"Great, now I'm going to have to ponder on that too," Miles told him.

The next few days were spent refining the Autotelekinetic Cantrip plan he was working on, the so-called 'Equilibrium' enhancement. Writing down every aspect of it, and giving it a name as well. Enhanced Mobile Marksmanship. Heightened Muscle Memory Learning. A big one was 'Telekinetic Nudge,' that apparently would use The Aura's power to bump an object just right, and also with enough subtlety to make it seem natural. The first test was on a roulette wheel set up in the Holographic Arena, where the Telekinetic Nudge would make the ball bounce just right to land in the number he wanted, but with no visible outright changes in its directions and speed. That was the single most difficult part, refining the Telekinetic Nudge, and even after the time he had spent working on it, it still wasn't entirely ironed out. This one was going to take a while.

A knock on his door. Seemed a little different from Arakai, though. Sure enough, when Miles opened it, it was Micah Jorvask, Jarrek's courier for their meeting on Redaria Prime.

"Oh... Micah, was it?" Miles asked, and she nodded. "Did you need something?"

"Personal project, thought you could help. You seem intuitively minded enough for it," Micah explained.

"I'm listening."

Micah placed a projector on the table in the dining room, which showed a 3-D model of a solid stone fortress. "The Velani Militarium has been wanting to build a sort of 'training base' for quite some time now. A great massive fort to send recruits, soldiers, officers, whatever for the purpose of... well, general training. Living there on-demand and as needed, a rotating contingent from the system's armed forces."

The Velani Militarium was the name of the joint armed forces of the Velani Array solar system, which included Redaria Prime, Redaria Omega, Laksor, and a binary planet system, Koros-Nathineyl.

"But it seems there's nowhere in all of the Velani Array system that actually meets what we'd need. Not least of all, just the space to put a fort like this."

"I haven't got any ideas right now, but I'll keep my eyes open. Did you consider Zharekk, perhaps Maybe the Haji-Son outlier planet of Homphalion?"

"We did, but Zharekk's a nightmare of a planet to build stuff on. Sure, once it's done, it's there for good, but getting there... no, don't care to deal with *that* much grief from nature."

Micah sat down at the table, and grumbled slightly, presumably at how frustrating it was to scout for a suitable location for this fortress.

"As for Homphalion, if it weren't for how many other bids were going on those mountain plateaus, we'd do it," Micah grumbled.

"Would a drink help?" Miles asked, and she nodded. "Hot or cold?"

Micah thought for a minute, resting her chin on the table. "Hot."

Miles prepared some hot water and grabbed a few leaves from a plant that was at this point, a keepsake from Earth as much as a chocolate mint plant.

"I remember growing these back on Earth. They're startlingly low-maintenance," Miles said as he tossed a generous few leaves into the boiling water, and letting it roll for a few minutes before turning the heat off.

"You seem to have a strange variety of skills,"

Micah commented. "I've heard of your training in martial arts, the prowess you've earned in battle against Demons, the tactics you employed at New Tacoma, and you're apparently also a regular musician at the Drowning Sorrows in Kaldres-Viane. To top it off, you can cook, and also are clearly knowledgeable on sourcing your own ingredients, and their maintenance as well."

Miles finished brewing the light tea and set a mug in front of Micah, and one for himself.

"I mean, I get that specialization might be for insects, but most everyone, hell, *all* everyone I've known can stick with something they're really good at, and live perfectly well. And sure, dabbling in other stuff... but... you've got those skills like they were all supposed to be your way of life," Micah continued.

"Micah, among the most frequent questions I asked on Earth was 'what the fuck do you want from me?'" Miles said with a sigh. "People with only a sliver of the skill I could muster were having twice the success, all because they were in the right place at the right time, and not least of all because they were older than me. The seniority complex on Earth is... staggering, and that's an understatement."

Both sipped their drinks, but not simultaneously. Miles specifically waited for a beat after Micah raised her mug.

"Even running that traveler's stop, I wasn't profiting by a long shot. If it weren't for The Aura, and the fact I could use it to just will some gold bars into existence, it would've crashed and burned." Miles then laughed. "My timing, comically rotten. My life before The Aura, utterly not worth mention. At all. And from it, I've developed an absolute disgust for luck. Fuck luck. Luck is just bullshit when it works in your favor."

Miles then sighed again. "Sorry, you didn't come here to hear me rant. You came here to—"

"It's fine," Micah said. "I didn't come here for tea either, but I got that, and I'm not complaining."

Miles nodded. "I'll keep an eye out for a good place for that fort."

"I know."

After Micah took her leave, Miles slumped back in his chair and groaned, needing to let off some steam, and taking the Aura Runner back to Fortem Terra Nova. This time, he landed in Third Orleans.

"I swear, whoever named this place has a deliberate lack of taste," Miles commented upon seeing that the name wasn't New New Orleans. A few scans around with The Sight later, and he found what he was after.

"Gentlemen, a moment?" Miles piped up to a trio that The Aura's Sight and borderline clairvoyance informed him each had outstanding bounties for assaults, rapes and worse.

"The fuck's this guy want?" one of them scoffed.

"Let's not beat around the bush, we all know," Miles said, staring down the one on the left.

The man on the right nodded, and without breaking eye contact with the one on the left, Miles kicked the unsuspecting scum hard in the solar plexus, leaving him gasping for air that could hardly be found, and the other two startled for a half-moment, allowing Miles the time to jab the man he had been staring down, and block the inbound haymaker from the only person to not have been injured thus far. A couple of elbow strikes rectified this quickly, and Miles was ready to see the one who started on the right get over the light stun of being jabbed in the nose.

But he was almost disappointed, as not only was he down for the count, the other two were also completely incapacitated. The trash he had kicked was now spitting up blood and his lunch, and the filth he introduced to his elbow was out cold.

"That's... really pathetic, guys," Miles commented as a patrol car closed in and the uniformed individual, identified as Orleans Internal Defense stepped out demanded he step away.

"Sir, these are Kenneth Hewer, John Zachary and

Guyvus P'Torn. If you've been paying attention to your APBs, you know what they're guilty of."

"Stand back, no moves," Miles was told, and he cooperated. The Guardsman grabbed his phone and checked the names, and faces, and then nodded.

"I'd've preferred it if you called in, and let us handle it from there."

"You can forego the reward if that forgives the transgression. I admittedly needed to get some exercise."

The two looked at the three men still wincing and writhing on the ground. The one who had been 'only' jabbed was finally collecting himself, then realized he was done for, and didn't bother to do much else.

"Yeah, I'm a little disappointed too," Miles added. "All yours."

"Fine, get outta here. Long as you're not in sight when the backup arrives, I can take the bounty if you insist, which you seem to."

Miles nodded and walked off towards a grocery store for something strongly caffeinated. After acquiring the can of brain fuel, gears started to turn in his head. The Conclave should be keeping a close eye on who they let leave Earth. And though the system wouldn't be foolproof, and sure, there'd be people who manage to leave who shouldn't, it seemed odd that they'd be able to last very long, let alone long enough to get back into the loop of wretchedness. It was most likely, however, that the newest generations of shitty Humans may have arisen from the latter half of two possibilities upon being given a whole new world: Either they'd use all that newness to get everything right, or even more enthusiastically wreck the place. Human nature, as Miles knew well, erred more towards that latter. It would fall to those who took the former path to set them straight, or bury them, lest they be buried.

"The iron reign doesn't come from the fall of the defense, or the surrender of good men. It comes because all everyone else wanted to do in their complacency was debate and compromise. And of course, the ones willing to destroy their foes will always win," Miles said to himself upon his conclusion. "And that goes both ways, in all its wonderful conflict."

In that instant, Miles remembered something.

"There's still one left. No wonder I still don't feel at peace."

Then, he defied one of the unwritten rules of the civilized universe and teleported directly from one planet to another.

Earth still looked startlingly the same from when he left it. Some cities might be worse for wear, but overall, not much had changed. Techbooth was still on

Cynofrax, and it could help him here once again.

"Techbooth, find Justice Emila Stantwell." Miles said this coldly, knowing that what he was about to do had been a long time coming. Something he had fantasized about for years before he even possessed The Aura. He sure hoped someone else hadn't beaten him to it. Then, the reply. A street address, an image of his target, and the house at that location.

"Confirm target presence?"

"Confirmed."

"Disable the house's security measures, if there's a checkback signal or something on the general house alarm, send a decoy signal of appropriate level and interval."

"Confirmed."

Techbooth's electronic voice was just as emotionless as Miles was at this moment. Emotion would come later, and he wasn't even sure which ones would show up when.

Miles knocked on the door, and the woman he despised for years answered.

"Who are you?" she asked.

"You don't know," Miles stated. "You wouldn't care to know."

A blast of The Aura later, and Emila was catapulted back into a wall, barely able to gasp for breath and reaching for the panic alarm. No noise, no response from the panel.

"I want you to understand that won't work, and you are helpless," Miles said with no emotion to be found but seething fury. He then telekinetically locked the doors and windows. "You cannot escape, nor will you. You are at the mercy of someone who has already made up their mind and chosen what will be done about you, and nothing you can say or do will convince them otherwise."

Finally, Emila managed to speak. "Please, don't! I won't commit anyone again if that's what you want! Ever!"

"How dare you!" Miles shouted, and the rage that had been rising was now here to make itself known. "How fucking dare you say those words to me! How many other people begged like you do now, and you never listened?! You don't know! You didn't count! You know none of our names!"

Miles punched her in the gut, and her whole body lifted itself a few inches off the ground as she groaned and clutched her now-scrambled stomach.

"You need to understand in every fiber of your being that you are going to die, you are going to die painfully, and there is nothing you can do to stop it! No amount of begging, no offer of any kind will grant you a second less of the pain you are about to feel! And however much it is, it can never be enough! You can never suffer enough! You will never suffer enough in all of Time!"

Emila Stantwell had no words. Karma had reared its head at last, and only now was she realizing it.

Far across the universe, Veralis Stratenheim felt that something was dreadfully wrong, and Miles Radien was at the heart of the flood. She noticed that the Aura Runner, however, was still landed outside their home on Cynofrax, meaning that Miles had warped directly to Earth.

"There's only two things that Miles would *warp* back to Earth for. And there's no Demonic presence there now."

In her personal ship, the Celestial Dart, the warp took three days. The Aura Runner was a ship of myth before it was in Radien's hands, and such a trip was but a few hours for it. But she did not possess the Chronokey, he did. The only reason she didn't warp herself was because Miles was still in perfect physical health, and she could sense that with her own power. And as long as that was the case, she could wait, however much it made her dread. She did wait, and she did dread what might be happening.

Miles heard a knock on the door of Emila

Stantwell's home, and was ready for battle. But when The Aura's Sight told him it was Veralis, he calmed down.

"I'm not about to question why you're here," Miles said. "My business has concluded, however."

Veralis could sense an unnerving satisfaction about him. Like something he had longed to do for many years just took place, but revenge lay at its heart.

"What was it?" she finally asked.

"Personal."

Miles walked towards the Celestial Dart, ready to return to Cynofrax the proper way, but Veralis piped up once she saw an odd vat-like structure inside the house, just large enough to fit a Human and then some.

"What else is in there?"

"Salt," Miles said. "It takes five days without it, three days with."

Not a single word was said through the first day of the warp back to Cynofrax, before Miles spoke to Veralis first.

"I hope this isn't you picking me up after a mess I've made. Because there is no mess."

"I know," Veralis replied. "But I don't know if what you did was right. Normally I do, and from what I know of you, you wouldn't do something like this without a very specific, and burning reason."

"Remember when you wondered how I didn't go

mad back on Earth, and I asked you if you were sure I hadn't?"

Veralis nodded.

"That was the last link of that chain. I can hardly believe I forgot about it. I always knew that I wouldn't feel ecstatic about my revenge on her, but I certainly know that I will never be ashamed. It really just is... satisfaction, of a dream set in motion long ago. And what's wrong is that the dream was made to exist."

"Radien, I have no trouble betting that a Human could dream of skinning someone alive and throwing their body into a vat of salt and waiting for them to die of dehydration before bleeding out, but not you. Not Miles Sorvenjar Radien."

"I know. Because I also encased the vat in a Hyperbolic Chronofield to extend the conscious amount of passed time to three months for her."

Veralis was truly taken aback by this. She didn't gasp or sigh, she couldn't even figure what even a reaction to this could be. "Who was she?! What did she do that made you want this much revenge?!"

"The consequence of the crime of existing at a younger age than the person deciding your fate!" Miles snapped. "My time, my past on Earth is worth no mention, no celebration, and no pity! Now, that is assured! The taste of revenge may be called bittersweet, but I enjoy dark chocolate and beer, so what the hell do they know?!"

"This, I think may be your darkest hour, Radien."

"No, Veralis," Miles said with genuine sorrow and waning rage. "That was the hour that put my fate in hands that were full of bias and prejudice."

A moment passed in silence as Veralis sighed again, realizing that was the truth.

"Today was the final act of the angry little man that was Miles. He can finally rest now, never to return. I can finally move on, and live my life as the Miles Sorvenjar Radien you deserve to know instead. I'm sorry that this is what had to happen, and that you had to see me like this."

"I'd say something like 'not as sorry as she was,' or 'I'm sorry that you're right,' but I know that's not what would help any of us," Veralis said, turning on the Celestial Dart's autopilot and turning to Miles. "Because first off, I'd bet that if she was sorry, you wouldn't have done as much as you had, and second off, I can tell you've had enough moments of hating how right you were that you don't need me to say it."

"Thank you, Veralis," Miles genuinely said, then chuckled for a bit in a sort of cathartic nihilism. "You are honestly impossible. And I mean that in every compliment it can be. I would never think someone like you could exist, if it weren't for the fact that I met you."

"Is there... anything you might need?" she asked. Miles shook his head.

"No, you've done more than I can deserve already. Do what you wish, whether shun me, or test me, or just keep distance for some time. I will understand."

"And what if I wanted to comfort you instead?"

"Well, that would be the day," Miles said solemnly. Veralis shook her head and grabbed his arm, pulling him into her arms, to his utter shock. And in being so stunned, Miles couldn't bring himself to stop her. A few seconds later, Veralis finally released him, and Miles simply wore a confused look on his face, like he had just beheld something that broke the very foundations of the laws of reality.

"I... I will have to ponder on this," Miles said, heading back into the Celestial Dart's bunks for the rest of the trip.

In his head did the meeting with the Effigy take place. Miles entered a sort of 'canvas realm' that he projected them both into.

"That didn't make sense," Miles said. "That... just didn't make sense. Things don't work like that. I don't understand!"

He and the Effigy sat down.

"The oldest truth is that Radien stands alone,"

Miles reiterated. "That's how it works. That's how I work. It falls to me alone to fight my battles, to conquer my trials. That is the essence of how I must operate."

After a moment of thinking, Miles righted himself. "Today was an odd day, and flukes would not be beyond possibility," he said with resolve. "The Demon of my past is dead at long last, and that brings me peace. So I have conquered my trial. And that is good."

Miles dismissed the Effigy, and 'woke up' as the Celestial Dart landed on Cynofrax.

ACT III
THE KEYSTONE FUNDAMENT

'm not typically one to question something that has done nothing but work, but I seem to recall you telling me once that the Keystone Forge we possess was not easy to acquire."

Miles wondered this aloud as he and Veralis worked on their own separate projects in the workshop of their home.

"Keystone Forges are exceptionally rare, given the respective rarity of what makes it all work," Veralis replied. "Also, why are you only making parts with the Forge? You know you can just make the whole sum with the Matter Projector."

"Well, very few things beat the feeling of assembling something, switching it on, and hearing the whirring victory of the fruits of your labor," Miles replied. "And of course, admiring the whole assembly from two paces back, that you just accomplished. I played with

Legos quite a lot in my youth."

Veralis raised an eyebrow.

"Construction toy. The name translates to 'I assemble' or 'I create,' roughly."

Veralis nodded and continued programming the Forge. Miles carefully snapped together a few parts to an improvement for the scope of his Orvitarian Collapse Rifle, a very intense look of concentration on his face.

"I remember a very wise man once telling me that if you can just snap your fingers and create a dozen explosive barrels and ragdolls to strew across them, the resulting spectacle is about as satisfying as eating your own snot," Miles added. "By the same token, of course, satisfaction comes provided your processes are successful. So I'll gladly leave the true minutia to the Forge. Microchips and programming, what have you. Putting all together like Legos... is what makes it all... work!"

As he spoke, Miles placed together the last parts of the module, and attached it to the scope, then looked through it to see if what he was working on was successful.

"Turn on that fan over there?" Miles asked, and Veralis did.

"Yes... yes! I will take that!" It seemed that the scope improvement worked.

"So, what is it, then?" Veralis asked.

"I've installed a laser distance gauge to the scope, exact to up to five thousand meters, and a wind reader, both tuned to the adjustment dials for automatic calculation of how to compensate for them. Of course, there's a readout of the distance, windage and direction as well. But I very deliberately have made it *not* actually do those corrections for you."

Veralis seemed perplexed by this, and Miles was quick to explain. "If all I have to do is point and pull, I don't learn a damn thing. I gain no skill, and spend no effort. An empty victory, which is no victory at all. Besides, there's no way to reliably tell the software to mark a given target for those automatic corrections."

The scope shunted back into the rifle's assembly for its easier transport and carry.

"You seem to value learning highly," Veralis noted.

"I mean... yeah, I guess I do," Miles realized. "Sure it seems obvious now, even to me, but I never really properly noticed that I do genuinely value the acquisition of skill, and the bettering of oneself through skill and learning."

With that project finished, Miles went over to a layout of the 'Equilibrium' plan he had with passive enhancements via The Aura. He was about to write something down, when his comm-link pinged. It was Dorg, the Hykentiu representative of the species's major planets in the Conclave of Sentience.

"Dorg?" Miles tentatively asked, unsure entirely if he was remembering the name correctly.

"Aye, that's me. Miirkae's here as well," Dorg replied, followed by a greeting from offscreen, presumably from Miirkae, the warrior from Pogo-Pira that Miles was acquainted with. "There's been a landmark discovery that warrants a meeting of several species, and since the rest of the Humans don't entirely care about Conclave matters, I figured you might at least want to know."

"Uh... is it—" Miles started hesitantly.

"Not at all! In fact, there's a lot of excitement about it. You'll be briefed on Turazin if you decide to attend."

Miles nodded, saying he'd be there, then hung up. "Knowledge and learning, eh?" he then said to Veralis, who laughed in agreement.

When Miles arrived on Turazin, the atmosphere was indeed one of excitement. It was nice to know that there were still new things that even a universe as advanced as this one could get eager over learning.

Representatives from over a hundred solar systems were present, and Miles was among some of the

<GREGOR FJELLREV>

independent parties of interest. A silver-scaled Draconian went up to the stage, to make what could only be an announcement he was happy to tell.

"As many of you are likely aware, a new Keystone Gem has been discovered on the planet of Korvideyl. And for those who are not aware, a new Keystone Gem has been discovered on the crystal planet of Korvideyl."

A hush fell over the crowd. Miles had heard of the planet Korvideyl, whose surface was dotted with caves filled with unique crystal stones, some with psionic tendencies ranging from the benign to the very specifically powerful, that ran through and across the planet like the living blood vessels of the world.

"The Korvideyl Optima Geode, as we've come to call it, is among the largest and most pristine Keystone Gems we have ever encountered. Its study will give great insight into these incredible gems, and we may even yet discern the Keystone Fundament from this very Geode."

This was followed by gasps of speculation and questions of potential hubris. The Keystone Fundament seemed, especially to Miles, something that really didn't have a tangible answer. The question being, what fundamental principle the Keystone Gems operated on, that allowed them to treat matter, energy and information all as one, and could manipulate one to another. The rest of this announcement went well enough, and the Optima Geode would be kept at Korvideyl Station, which was based on the planet's single moon. Of course, people would be allowed to study it, and all research and information gathered would be compiled into a single openly-accessible repository for review and further study.

"If we have unearthed one of the most powerful and pristine Keystone Gems in history, there's gonna be plenty more players involved in wanting it under their control," Miles admitted to himself. It was only at this point that he noticed that the Redarian Micah Jorvask was standing near to him, and he noticed by her nodding in agreement.

"Aye, it quite honestly makes me suspicious that Korvideyl's research body would so openly admit a new Keystone Gems's existence. Considering the sensitive nature of such artifacts, one would think they'd want to not draw attention to themselves as they discerned just how powerful this Optima Geode is."

Miles looked over to Micah, wondering just how she managed to sneak into this crowd without him noticing.

"I'll ask how how you know so much about Keystone Gems later, but I agree. To announce the potential discerning of the Keystone Fundament is a volatile subject, one that would garner a hell of a lot of unwanted attention, especially considering the recent incursions by the Burning Hells, and the introduction of the Humans to the universe. It makes me suspicious why Korvideyl's scientific body would be so quick to say that they found it."

Both Micah and Miles stood for a moment, pondering their next action.

"I'll study the Geode itself," Micah started.

"I'll learn more of this Draconian," Miles finished.

The Draconian, of the Nuvenr Genetic Caste, his name was Kor-Vas-Tarn, roughly translating to 'He who learns' from the Nuvenr form of the Draconian language. Unlike the Bol'Drakkin, the Nuvenr were considerably taller when standing on two legs, but usually preferred to opt for remaining on all fours due to their rather long bodies, only ever rearing up if the need to intimidate should arise. Kor-Vas-Tarn, as it turned out, was a veteran scientist from Korvideyl station, and his credentials were surely solid. It even made sense that he would be quick to announce the finding of a Keystone Gem on Korvideyl. Miles soon decided he should pay a visit to the Crystal Planet itself.

Upon arriving at Korvideyl's moon station, Miles met up with Kor-Vas-Tarn, happening to run into him in one of the corridors.

"Think you could walk with me for a bit? I've got a

bit more than my back can reasonably take." Kor-Vas-Tarn was on all fours like back on Turazin, where his announcement was made, and along his back were strapped several bags with research binders and the like. Miles grabbed one of the bags, and the Nuvenr Dragon thanked him as they continued to walk.

"I'm just gonna process something I've figured out real quick, but do feel free to chime in if you find yourself able," he continued, and Miles nodded. "One of the undiscerned caverns has been cleared for exploration and categorization, and I'd go down if it weren't for how many people are bugging me about the Optima Geode. That said, if that cavern isn't mapped now, it likely won't be for decades to come as work piles up."

"Perhaps you're owed a break. There's a standard process for undiscerned caverns, I'd imagine?" Miles suggested.

"Where did you transfer from?" Kor-Vas-Tarn asked. "You clearly didn't get here that long ago."

"Laksor Gentech. The GAMA's nice and all, but tedious as hell and doesn't even have the benefit of being fieldwork." Miles quickly answered, essentially winging it and figuring that Jaden would vouch for him if it came to that. But the answer was quick enough that Kor-Vas-Tarn just nodded and said, 'I get that.'

"Regardless, with the Optima Geode taking up so

much time being new and interesting, perhaps you might figure that cavern as a break from it. Being able to go through the paces will likely be a refreshing change from having to be clever in new ways all the time." Miles continued.

"You're honestly right," Kor-Vas-Tarn replied, opening the door to his personal quarters. "Just on that end table there."

Miles set down the satchel on the table, and Kor-Vas-Tarn started to unpack that and the other packs he was carrying.

"I'll probably take tomorrow to map out that cavern, then," Kor-Vas-Tarn decided.

"Solid plan. It gets tiring as hell to constantly be getting cleverer and cleverer."

Kor-Vas-Tarn looked over to Miles. "You're correct. But you seem a bit young to have that understanding in your voice. Did you have to grow up too fast?"

Miles was taken aback by this. "Well yikes, dude. Hittin' hard and fast on that one."

"I apologize, then."

"No, it's all right. The answer to that question is I don't know. All I know is that I grew up, not if it was too fast, or if it should or shouldn't have been that way. I'll have to ponder on that."

"I think you should take a break to go through some paces you know well, after all, it gets tiring as hell to constantly be getting cleverer and cleverer."

Miles soon found himself at one of the station's Sustenance Wings. It was called a Sustenance Wing, but in all honesty, that was just the more scientific way of saying restaurant and bar.

"Are the Nuvenr known for weapons-grade intuition?" Miles asked the barkeep after asking for something potent to drink.

The Kanikai barkeep laughed. "Oh boy, if I had an iron nail for every time I heard someone say that after talking to Kor-Vas-Tarn, I could build a city from the metal." This Kanikai was of a breed that made him almost Loriken in appearance, like a Siberian Husky's close appearance to wolves. "Nuvenr Draconians are known for having very fast-processing brains. Sometimes it manifests as an uncanny sort of intuition."

The rest of that night was relatively uneventful. Miles had come to learn of the Draconian who announced the Optima Geode's existence, but hadn't intended it like *that*. After having a spare quarters assigned to him, Miles flopped on the bed and just laid there.

"For some reason, even though I know I don't need to sleep, I still can't help but want to flop on a bed and just stay there for a bit," he admitted to himself.

Someone knocked on the door, and Miles sprang up to check who it was, and answer once he saw that it was Micah.

"Find anything?" Miles asked.

Micah shrugged. "Nothing people don't already know, maybe we're looking in the wrong spot for trouble."

"Maybe we don't need to be looking at all," Miles responded. "I think we both know why we're concerned. The Humans are out and about in the universe, and we have access to their history books. I understand that's why I'm worried about the announcement so soon. It makes sense that Kor-Vas-Tarn would make such an ambitious move, considering both the size of the Geode, its potency, and the fact of his dedication to researching the Keystone Gems. Hell, he might even later quietly back off of his statement about the Keystone Fundament. It all lines up."

Micah sighed in agreement. "Yup. Honestly, yup. Radien, if anyone trusts the Humans less than you, it's myself and Jarrek. And between him and I, Jarrek's the one with proper foundation for it, having been to Earth for a bit..."

Micah then flopped on the bed that Miles had only just vacated with a slight grumble. He didn't mind,

<FIRE TO BURN THE STARS>

not like he needed it.

"Honestly, this is something I'm willing to let be alone until something happens. The Humans weren't even too interested in this, according to Dorg. And honestly? I don't anticipate them becoming so, given that the buzz will likely die down before they can start really involving themselves in the intergalactic community," Miles concluded, to which Micah processed for a bit, then nodded. She then patted the bed a few times with her handpaw, like one might encourage a cat to come sit on your lap. Miles was very confused.

"Oh, Redarians are generally a pretty cuddly species, and I'm no exception," Micah explained. Miles froze.

"But you would want to... with me? And you're just so quick to make that known?"

Micah stood up and looked at Miles, then tilted her head a little, like she was studying him, before looking directly into his eyes, and then made an audibly surprised sigh.

"Gods... Spiteforged..." she said, and her tone was almost pained.

"The what now?"

Micah sat down at the small table in the quarters, and motioned for Miles to sit across from her. "Redaria used to have this weird sort of caste system. We've long since abandoned it, it was based on what kind of person you were by the time you reached adulthood. You lived your natural course of life up till then, and then you were assigned to whatever way of life you were based on the kind of person you became. A lot of the ideas from this have also been abandoned, but one word has stuck around to describe a very particular kind of person. That word is Spiteforged."

Miles grabbed himself a drink, he figured he'd need it for this one.

"Hard to properly define, but you sure knew one when you met 'em. Some other names included the Denied, the World-Betrayed, the Sparkstolen... I'll bet you've never heard a casual compliment in your life up to the very moment I suggested an overnight snuggle?"

Miles nodded simply. It was a fact of his life, and since hating fact doesn't change it, no sense in letting it affect you if you can help it. And Miles could indeed help it.

"Every praise or validation you ever heard was just from obligation, or was prompted because you said something that made idiots worry?"

Miles nodded again, but slower, and with his eyes narrowed in suspicion.

"Say you were discussing an idea for a story or game with someone, and they may have been listening, sure, but you couldn't help but feel like you were just taking up space? And when you asked if there were better things to talk about, they'd just say 'No, no, it's fine! It's a good idea!' and what have you? And exactly in that sort of obligated tone?"

Miles stopped and just stared, his gaze cold and hard.

"Everyone was always 'just saying that.'"

Miles stood up sharply, turning around with the empty bottle in his hand about to throw it at the wall away from them, but he barely held himself back, setting it back down on the table and looking over to Micah.

"Don't try to decode me, Micah. I'm not a puzzle to be solved or a challenge to be figured out," Miles said calmly.

"Radien, I'm not a Human. I don't care to know how every one of those gears in your head turn, which way they spin and what tactics they produce. But by the same token, I'm not a Human, and I don't want to see a good man burn."

Miles froze for almost a full minute. His next words quivered as he forced himself to confess. "Micah... no one's ever called me a man before, let alone a... good one..."

Micah rushed over and caught Miles before he would've fallen to his knees over this and, with a lot more strength than her stature might suggest, carried him over to the bed in the quarters and laid on top of him.

Miles's breath was slow and controlled as he carefully put a hand across Micah's shoulders. "Why did you catch me?"

"Because you were falling."

When morning came around, he only then noticed he had actually fallen asleep during the night. The Aura made it so that he didn't need to, but it didn't make him unable to, as proven by this. Micah woke up not long after with a yawn, soon getting up and stretching.

"I'm planning on having a chat with Kor-Vas-Tarn, he is an old colleague of mine, after all. Besides, I want to study the Optima Geode anyway," Micah said while stretching herself out, and then hitting a button on a nearby wall panel to get the sustenance replicator to make a cup of... well, it didn't look like coffee, but it was probably similar in purpose. Miles nodded, and just before she headed off, Micah looked back to him, clearly as he was in the middle of pondering, and likely regretting.

"Radien... I understand on a factual level why you're probably... primordially confused right now, even though I can't relate. I wish I could tell you something useful, something enlightening, but all I, and more people than you might realize can do is hope you figure it out, since I know you'll need to figure it out yourself." Micah said understandingly.

Miles looked up to her. "That was a useful thing to say, Micah. Thank you."

Micah nodded, and headed out, soon chatting up one of the Corvuseine scientists, an avian-type species hailing from the planet of !leysa (the name pronounced as a click of the tongue followed by 'leysa'), leaving Miles to his thoughts.

He closed his eyes and summoned the Effigy.

"I'm... at a loss for words," Miles started. "I just don't get it. At all." But there wasn't much to finish with, so he just stood there as the Effigy sat.

"What even *can* I think about this? I can't ask what I *do* think, because this isn't something I've ever even considered the existence of, let alone thinking about it. I just don't get it."

Miles then sat down across from the Effigy, who listened silently as always.

"There's gotta be something you have, right? Something you can tell me? Some kind of advice, or anything at all?"

A moment passed.

"No, of course not. You're a projection of my mind's eye, so you only have my knowledge. And I don't have knowledge on this. My knowledge doesn't go this far. How the hell do I even deal with that, then? I guess I'll just keep moving forward, call that another fluke—"

The whole station suddenly shook, as if rattled from an explosion, and Miles stood up, dismissing the Effigy and walking out of his room.

"Are there tectonic quakes on this moon?" he asked of his next-quarters neighbor, who shook his head. At the same time Miles checked a nearby terminal, an alarm blared, signaling an external breach. Something just blew a hole in Korvideyl station from the outside.

Miles rushed over towards the area, and Micah was already leading people away from there, along with several other cooler-headed individuals. The blast wasn't far from Kor-Vas-Tarn's quarters, and the lab that the Optima Geode was being kept in.

Korvideyl Station's defenses were minimal, being a public science station. It was mostly oxygen shields for in case of such a rupture, and a small security staff. Likely no match for whoever just blew a hole in the wall.

Soon, Miles saw who he was dealing with. Humans, it had to be. They were in full body armor, with traditional rifles that weren't far from old Earth models. They were moving in, with their excess of gear and pitch black armor to appear like an enigma, trying to seem endless and faceless, but would undoubtedly throw a

<FIRE TO BURN THE STARS>

tantrum like a toddler if not handed absolute power on a silver platter. Humans indeed. All too Human.

Charging forward and slamming one of the assailants against the wall, Miles used the assistance of The Aura to telekinetically nudge bullet paths away from him, and evade the rest while beating the living daylights out of these chuds. He yanked the helmet off of one and smacked the same man with it, soon confirming the species he had suspected.

Micah slid in, low to the ground with a longsword, lopping off the foot of a Human attacker, and quickly slicing his throat open before using her blade to control the barrel of her next opponent's rifle, and stick her knife up their throat.

Only now did Miles conjure forth the Borfblade, slicing it through his next quarry's weapon as they tried to ram him with it, the cutlass also cutting through their chin. Miles then quickly finished them off by driving the sword through their chest, and moving on to the next.

The last few armed goons opened fire, spraying bullets at the two, but Miles held out his hand and created a shield with The Aura, that stopped the rounds before they would've even gotten too close for comfort. With a flip of his wrist, those bullets then shredded all but one, leaving him gasping for what was left of life.

Miles then heard a door open, the one to Kor-Vas-

Tarn's quarters, where it seemed a few of the Human invaders had gotten to. Definitely the past tense *had*, since out was thrown two bodies like ragdolls, and another guttural scream as the Nuvenr Dragon showed the less nicer side of his race by way of tooth and claw.

Miles held out his hand, sustaining the sole Human survivor's life, intending to question him.

"What were you after here? And why did you figure you had to forcibly invade a *public science station* to get it?!"

The Human spat, and chomped on what must have been a cyanide tooth. Miles of course, yanked the poison out of his mouth with his power, to the shock and clear disturbance of this fool who thought he could take the easy way out.

"My best advice is to answer questions truthfully, because the facts will be out one way or another. By you saying them, or by pulling the information out of your living brain. Your choice, though," Miles left off with as the man was restrained and taken away by a Corvuseine guardsman and another Redarian scientist.

Miles then turned to Micah, and chuckled. "Did you see the look on his face when his fuckin' cyanide didn't work? Glorious."

Micah nodded in fairness, a little more relieved when she saw that despite the rather high injury count, there were no fatalities other than the Humans. "Nice fighting alongside you, Radien. We should do it again sometime, albeit with less collateral at risk."

The Human survivor by the name of Travis Shores was taken to Turazin for questioning, and Miles had requested to aid in the process, soon given first crack at it since despite being one of the slaughterers of Travis's team, he was from the same species.

"What were you gunning for from Korvideyl station?" Miles started with, to Travis's silence.

"Obviously. Look, I have no plans to be patient here, so I'm gonna be honest with you and tell you that the factual truth will be known one way or another. The use of telepathic extraction hasn't been done since the Essentium Wars of the Seventh Cosmic Era. We're currently in the eighth, for reference, and it'd be nice to keep that streak up."

Travis shook his head as Miles stood up and turned around to leave. "Why did they let you have all this knowledge? You so easily just know the history of the universe, what made you special?"

"Because I fucking asked!" Miles yelled, slamming his hands on the table. Travis almost jumped, but managed to keep himself from it. "It's the fucking equivalent of space Googling! This information isn't restricted, Korvideyl Station is a *public science facility!*

You could have knocked on the door, and they'd've let you in, no questions asked! It is *beyond* me why you figured you had to invade!"

Miles sighed. "It honestly doesn't matter to me what you choose, because everyone's gonna know the facts of the matter regardless, even the Humans still on Earth throwing hissy fits about having to give up their nukes. Your choice right now is how you, and by extension, the Human race is remembered today."

Miles turned around to walk out once again, when Travis spoke up.

"Why'd they send you?" he asked. "You slaughtered my team."

"Despite that fact, we all figured you'd talk to any Human before anyone else. If you want to improve what the universe thinks of you and your species, prove them wrong on that."

Miles left the room after that, about an hour later learning that Travis had told Xenidar everything once it was his turn, to Miles's surprise.

Apparently, the Humans of Fortem Terra Nova had created a paramilitary called SWEEPS, whose purpose was to acquire and study off-Earth technologies for the use of Earth's Empire, as it seemed to be calling itself. They didn't even have an emperor elect, but they certainly seemed united in a goal to be shitty. The attack on Korvideyl Station was an attempt to acquire the Optima Geode for study and use in that vein, having used operatives who lied their way off of Earth by answering the moral tests 'correctly,' as it were, saying what needed to be said as a means to that end. Xenidar later met up with Miles.

"It's so odd. I mean, the Conclave has had to introduce troubled races to the universe before, but the Humans... it's like... other races were troubled because they didn't have all the facts or knowledge. But I have never before encountered a species that would outright reject and denounce fact simply because it doesn't fit their view of how things work. You could bring a Human proof, hard proof of a given fact, and they'd slap it out of your hand and insult you because it's not their spoon-fed viewpoint on reality. It is unfathomable," Xenidar said after explaining to Miles the results with Travis. "That Travis fellow... I think he only told me what he did because you said history was gonna remember him regardless, and he went for the one where history would like him better."

"Welcome to Humans," Miles said, raising his glass and drinking enthusiastically from it. "They're psychologically hardwired to reject fact that doesn't fit their worldview. And I don't just mean 'them's the facts' facts. I mean, the literal phenomenon of factual truth.

They are predisposed to reject it if it doesn't fit neatly into how they think things work... and I'm not an exception."

Xenidar seemed confused by this.

"Humans twist fact to fit theory, that's how they work. And unfortunately, I'm honestly not immune to that," Miles clarified.

Xenidar raised an eyebrow and Miles soon comforted him by saying that he'd be counting on having his head put on a pike if he indeed walked down a darker path for that fact of himself.

"I'd be more concerned if you thought yourself the exception, Radien."

Both laughed at this, despite the implications of the day's events. SWEEPS seemed to be the new looming threat, and there was no way the fight could be taken to Earth. Even Miles would have his hands rather tied on the matter, since he wasn't considered to be from Earth anymore, even by the Humans both on and off it. At least, it seemed, no one would be trying to appeal to species loyalty in his travels. But Miles did get the lingering feeling that SWEEPS was going to be a consistent thorn in the shoulder, like how the Demons popped up every now and again, so might SWEEPS. It would at least keep him occupied, for sure.

Afterwards, Miles headed home. When he walked

through the door, he felt that something was off, though. As if he was walking into a trap. Keeping his vigilance, Miles went for the fridge to grab some ingredients to make himself a snack.

The pitter-patter of footsteps behind him was unmistakable. Miles threw his leg out behind him to side kick his attacker, but Veralis spun around his foot and evaded it, grabbing him from behind and heaving him across the room onto the couch in the adjacent area. After recovering his bearings, Miles stood up.

"Have you been reading Earth comic strips again?!" he shouted.

"I'm just saying, that Hobbes fellow was a genius."

Miles rolled his eyes and resumed his attempt to get something to eat, which thankfully went unimpeded. After successfully consuming the small snack, despite looking over his shoulder every now and again, met with Veralis sticking out her tongue with mischief, Miles received a ping from Turazin.

"Okay, what's your bet? I'm thinking Dorg," Miles guessed.

"Xenidar," Veralis predicted. "You just spoke with him not long ago, therefore you aren't expecting it to be Xenidar, so thus—"

"All right I get it." Miles opened the channel, and

tried to hide the visual feed from Veralis, because she was correct. But that alone gave her confirmation.

"I'm not interrupting, am I?" Xenidar asked, confused.

"No, you're good. Veralis is just being… Veralis," Miles said. "What do you need?"

"You… might want to come to Turazin to discuss. It's annoyingly complicated."

After arriving at The Hideout, Xenidar explained. "SWEEPS just set up a base about ten kilometers away from here."

"What the hell?! Shouldn't it be razed to the ground?!" Miles exclaimed, and Xenidar quickly cut in.

"Look, the problem is that by a frankly offensive amount of sheer technicalities, it's completely acceptable. There's no mandate that says that The Hideout and the Spire of the Conclave *have* to be the only two buildings on Turazin, SWEEPS's origin planet is Fortem Terra Nova, which means that it's not violating the selective sanctions on Earth, and there's really just no way anyone can take it down *until* they actually do something illegal. And I'll bet every man and woman in that base knows it. I've already made it very clear to everyone at The Hideout that they are not to be impeded in normal operations, and that we can't try to tempt them, or they'll know it."

Miles sighed. "I'm honestly not sure if I can accept that. That's how it *starts*, Xenidar. That's how it's started before on Earth. Their end goal is to be shitty, we gotta squash the cockroach before it starts a colony!"

"Radien, I'm not disagreeing with you," Xenidar said, then flicking his left ear towards one of the back rooms. "But right now, we have to put our best foot forward, and until something happens, nothing has happened. Now then, you may find one of the entries into the Manifest of Apocalypse interesting. Follow me."

Miles recognized the ear flick as a sort of trusting wink among the Vulpian species, and he nodded in agreement, before following Xenidar to the aforementioned back room, and the door closed. Xenidar pressed a button, waited a few seconds, then spoke.

"All right, now we can talk properly."

"You think the Humans have bugged The Hideout? It's a bit much credit to be giving them," Miles said.

"This extra step worked, didn't it? You got the message, and the one we wanted to send was delivered too, and if it turns out it wasn't needed, more power to us," Xenidar assured. "And you are right. This is indeed how it starts. Everyone knows it. In fact, everyone knows it so well that there's already an unspoken plan between us all. And the fact of the matter is, the Conclave isn't

<GREGOR FJELLREV>

responsible for internal matters within a species. Meaning if a Human wreaked hell on SWEEPS, the Conclave cannot be faulted."

"Even I'm a slippery slope," Miles admitted. "I'm not considered from Earth anymore, and the fact that I operate with the interests of the Conclave in mind almost ties my hands. Almost."

Miles then had an idea. "That said, I still think I might be able to make something happen, and I won't even be the Human who does it."

Back on Fortem Terra Nova, Ellan Hector was practicing his carpentry in New Tacoma.

"You can't dovetail Naldrimor Whitewood, it's too soft," a voice said from behind as he lined up the plank at the band saw.

"And you'd know?" Ellan said as he turned around to see Miles Radien.

"It's on a perfect equilibrium of hardness that makes it deceptive. Miter cut, sure. Plenty of artisans have been fooled before though, and the appeal is there, despite the fact that it looks like a somehow even plainer version of Oak."

"Yup, it's so risky to treat and work with that if you do manage to make something out of it, people pay a lot for it. Back on Earth, fugu didn't taste all that incredible, but the danger factor made it so valuable."

"Well, fortunately Naldrimor Whitewood venom is only painful and not lethal. Good to see you again, Ellan."

"You too. How can I help?"

Miles sat down with Ellan once he had finished setting up the gluing for the box he was making, and explained the situation with SWEEPS, as well as the fact that he knew there was more to Ellan than met the eye.

"SWEEPS doesn't even have a whole lot of favor here on Fortem Terra Nova," Ellan admitted. "And I suppose people like us can recognize each other. "But yes, even other people here know that SWEEPS is no good. If it weren't for the fact that I don't exactly have the gear to take them on, I'd bring the fight to Turazin myself."

"Today is your lucky day, then," Miles said, and Ellan raised an eyebrow. Was he actually going to get his chance at valor?

Miles then showed Ellan the Aura Runner, and an experimental technology he had been working on.

"I've called it the Tesla Key," Miles explained. "It's a sort of... frequency discerner and utilizer. Anything that operates on any kind of electronic signal at all, this thing can figure out the frequency of that signal, replicate it and use it, even send it into a system internally. Like when you punch in some numbers on a keypad, there's

<GREGOR FJELLREV>

somewhere in the keypad's programming that makes it remember the correct combination, and the Tesla Key can isolate it, then send that signal to open the door. Basically Tesla was right, and everything is frequencies. And even if they have manual locks on stuff, that's where the Needle Key attachment to the device comes in. Just stick the needle into a keyhole, and it takes a 3-D scan of the inside of the lock, then replicates a key to fit in that specific keyhole using Morphic Metal. This little device would probably be terrifyingly illegal if it became well-known."

Ellan studied the device, and nodded in approval. "I assume you'll want it back once I'm done?" Miles nodded to that, and they soon found themselves on Turazin, overlooking the SWEEPS base.

"Yeah, if you can get me in there, I can wreck 'em from within. And uh... I am curious, Miles," Ellan said after a study with high-power binoculars.

"Go on?"

"How have you known? It seems a bit too... serendipitous that suddenly a guy like me found himself in the company of you, of all people."

"I asked myself that same question when I met a Draconian named Melaqros all that time ago on Earth. But I can say that after all the frustration and grey that my life was up till then, I know when I see someone else

<FIRE TO BURN THE STARS>

who has lived the same way, and I never want anyone to live like that again if I can help it."

Ellan nodded, and then asked about getting inside.

"I've done a scan-pulse on the building, and fortunately they don't have instruments to detect such scan-pulses yet. So I do have the layout, and I'll be warping you into one of the personnel locker bays. First thing you should do is get a disguise as one of them, and the Tesla Key should be able to make that easy to do."

Ellan shook his head. "No, you can't warp me in. Even if a Human from Fortem Terra Nova destroyed this base, a warp-in would give it away that they had help from another species, that'd defeat the point. But with the Tesla Key, I could walk straight through the front door, posing as anyone I wanted to. That said..." Ellan then called up the map of the complex that was on the Tesla Key's screen. "There's a sort of 'employee entrance' near the west main garage. I could get in there plain-clothes and pick up whatever I needed once inside."

Miles quickly agreed with the plan, and Ellan soon moved out, entering the sensor range of the SWEEPS base from the western side. Miles watched on binoculars as he scanned the Tesla Key on the door, posing as security staff. The door opened, and Ellan walked in.

"Well, it's in his hands now," Miles commented, lowering the binoculars.

Now inside, Ellan began his work, casually walking past one of the armed guards, and swiftly jabbed him in the throat, then shoving him into a corner and continuing to strike the same area to ensure lethality. After taking what weapons and armor he found useful, Ellan then moved towards one of the weapons research ranges. It seemed most of the SWEEPS base was dedicated to researching weaponization possibilities for any non-human tech they could get their hands on. The irony was not lost on Ellan, considering some of the woodworking tools he possessed, he simply asked for and received without a fuss.

Miles noticed the lockdown and alarms that soon were raised, and sent Ellan a final message via telepathy.

"I'm getting out of here, can't risk implication. The device on your belt buckle will warp you over to The Hideout, and Xenidar is ready to move you into one of the safehouses."

Ellan heard, and muttered to himself "All right then, let's rock."

Exiting the small storage closet he had been gearing up in, Ellan moved out, raising his rifle at the approaching guards, and with the element of surprise, dropped them both with clean shots, and then one of the researchers that was with them when she reached for the weapon of the fallen guards. The last one started running, so Ellan let him be. It wasn't long after that the lockdown was beginning to take effect, and some of this experimental tech would need to be put into action early.

Ellan ducked into a side room, then noticed that on a small table there was a Redarian Bounce Knife, which had been mislabeled as "TARGET-SEEKING THROWING BLADE, UNKNOWN ORIGIN." He rolled his eyes, and grabbed the Bounce Knife, then opening the door and tossing it out, hurriedly re-closing it afterwards. Hearing both the sound of gunshots, confused shouts, metal on metal, metal on glass, metal on flesh followed by deathrattles, eventually Ellan opened the door again very slowly, and saw the Bounce Knife laying on the floor, spinning in place before settling.

"Yeah, even they weren't fond of using that one," he noted before moving on.

Miles paced about in The Hideout, and Xenidar had noticed.

"As much as that carpet is self-stitching, you might still manage to wear holes in it," he commented while reading a book. Specifically, Flora Valtarius's "The Manual of Exceptionally Advanced Tactics," the third in a series of fifteen. Flora Valtarius having been a well-known Taigron military leader, and overall really cool person. That said, her cookbook didn't do so well, as it was mostly bland, highly nutritious recipes for 'siege food,' as it were.

"Wouldn't be the first time," Miles replied, then heading over to a terminal out of curiosity, and looking to see if any Frigate-Class starships were registered under the name 'The Friggin Frigate.' To his satisfaction, eighty ships bore this name, most of them belonging to Lørkas Vulpian-run organizations. "I haven't heard of that chapter of the Vulpians before…"

"What, the Lørkas? They're… characters, to be sure," Xenidar noted, his voice thick with enough subtext one could likely cut it with a knife. Miles raised an eyebrow, then went back to killing time as Ellan killed the Humans at the SWEEPS base.

While Ellan wasn't having a hellish time at this task, it certainly was no picnic, and admittedly, SWEEPS was greatly underestimating the capabilities of both Ellan as a fighter, and the usefulness of the Tesla Key, which had rendered automatic defenses nonviable, as the Tesla Key could determine on what frequency the command codes operated on, then subsequently turn them on the frankly disturbing amount of military-grade guards present at a 'research facility.' The Tesla Key also ensured that no door was locked to Ellan, and most plans for

<FIRE TO BURN THE STARS>

cornering him relied on being able to lock doors.

"Oooh, I've wanted to try one of these for a while!" he said as soon as he saw some Draconian-made Pyrohelix Grenades in a box. It looked like SWEEPS had been grabbing as much non-human technology as they could get without questions asked, storing them rather haphazardly until species stopped handing over techs for free, *then* study and weaponize them, to Ellan's benefit, and their doom.

'Pinned' down in a corner again, Ellan activated the Pyrohelix Grenade he held, then chucked it down the hall. His eyes then widened as he noticed the wall he was using as cover was getting a bit too hot to handle, and retreated into a different room. When he walked back out into the hallway, there wasn't much hallway left, most of the affected structure melted or had completely vaporized.

"Oh, right. They were... meant to be able to burn Dragon scales. Yeah... okay, new rule, no more of those."

Meanwhile at The Hideout, Miles was ranting about how 'anti-fun' the Human cities on Fortem Terra Nova were in their naming, particularly with Third Orleans and York The Third, naming no city "New New York" or "New New Orleans." Xenidar had been listening for about the first third of the rant, before moving on to the fourth installment of Flora Valtarius's manuals, "The

Manual of Even More Exceptionally Advanced Tactics."

Ellan continued his one-man siege against SWEEPS, rounding a corner and reflexively slamming a man's head into the wall as he tried to take Ellan by surprise. Ellan subsequently commented on how he was glad his instincts were reliably sharp, then trying to discern the next phase of his plan, locking the doors that surrounded him so that he had time to think.

"If I blow this place to hell, then the Conclave gets involved because of an explosion on Turazin, regardless of where it was. If I depopulate it, then let's be honest, no one will think a Human alone did it. But in that case..."

The gears started to whir in Ellan's head, and soon he figured out exactly what his plan was. With the Tesla Key, he made his escape from the base. The damage was not irreparable, and the loss of life was not unrecoverable. The base was left in shambles more so than ruin, and the damage was within the plausible capabilities of a single clever Human from Fortem Terra Nova.

Ellan ducked into The Hideout's public library, and signaled to Miles via terminal that he had arrived. Miles soon led him to the bug-free room with Xenidar, who was reading the seventh book of Flora Valtarius's series, "The Manual of the Galaxy Brain Tactician."

"I think it went well," Ellan commented.

"I think the base is still there and will continue to be," Miles replied, not as disappointed as he was confused. He knew Ellan could've left a smoldering crater where the SWEEPS base once stood.

"Well, *I* think my plan will be to harass the base rather constantly, using The Hideout as a sort of staging ground for my one-man raids. If I can keep the Tesla Key here, the Humans will have to pay for every inch of ground they try to take. Besides, we all know where this SWEEPS base is. If I blew it up, we might not have the benefit of knowing where the next one will be built."

"The Ordslapp Principle," Xenidar commented, with a nod of approval. "The Hideout is yours to stay at for this purpose, Ellan."

"I'm sorry, the what now principle?" Ellan asked.

"There is a place on Cynofrax, Port Ordslapp, which is well-known as a dodgy smuggler's haven. But a clever few are aware that that's the point of its existence, its leadership basically rather intentionally is a bit lazy on tariff evasion and substance smuggling, which ends up ensuring that all these activities remain contained, more or less, to this one city. If and when Ordslapp *does* get its once-in-a-while slave trade ring, *that's* when the hammer drops, and drops hard," Miles explained. "Keeping the SWEEPS base standing because we know that's where SWEEPS will be is in the same general idea."

Ellan clarified that indeed, that was his reasoning. Miles decided to let Ellan keep the Tesla Key, and modified it slightly so if anyone other than Ellan attempted to use it, the device would deploy a 'shell' of electrified blades to deter prying eyes and hands alike. Ellan soon left for the 'room' that Xenidar had ready for him, which was more like a small house within The Hideout. Xenidar then turned to Miles.

"The Tesla Key, Radien," Xenidar started.

"What of it?"

"As much as Ellan has proven himself to be one of the good ones when it comes to Humans, I still must question the wisdom in even possessing such a technology, let alone giving it to a Human. It's practically a Keystone-level thing, operating on its own fundament, that fundament being frequency."

"It's not able to resonate a vault door into dust, Xenidar," Miles responded. "It's just a master key of sorts. Granted, no real such thing as *just* a master key. It's one of those things, I think, where it's just... Yes, it could be modified and repurposed into some kind of terrible new Artifact, but that's not what it was made for, and it might frankly be easier to just make the Artifact from scratch."

"Even so," Xenidar cautioned. "I don't even know

if I'd trust myself with something like the Tesla Key, and that might only be because of how many different things I can think of using it for, other than just opening doors and turning off cameras."

"Maybe that's what makes Ellan trustworthy to use it. Because right now, all he needs it for is opening doors and turning off cameras."

Miles then turned his attention to the comm-link in his pocket, which pinged with a message from Arakai.

PLANET: HOMPHALION

CITY: REYNVOL

COULD USE SOME HELP HERE

-ARAKAI

ACT IV
OF HELL AND VOID

As if it weren't bad enough that the Burning Hells want a piece of this universe!" Arakai shouted as he peeked his head out from cover, barely managing to get back down in time before a hail of seething purple-black bolts whizzed by.

He then looked over to where he sensed someone warping in nearby, and saw Miles Radien with his Collapse Rifle and Cutlass next to him in the cover.

"I hope I'm not the only person you called," Miles remarked. "What the hell are these guys? They sure don't look like Demons..."

"No, they're Voidspawns!" Arakai explained, lobbing what looked like a spool of wire over the cover and into the thick of it. The device then became a whirling ball of death, shredding through the titular creatures from beyond Reality.

"Well, it's bad enough that the Dark Six are a

thing…" Miles said, being met with a light bap from Arakai's handpaw for basically parroting him from earlier.

"Normally, the Voidspawns are kept busy by the Demons that try to break into the universe, this must mean there's a lull in the Burning Legions' numbers," Arakai noted. "But the overall goal of the lot is the same, make all reality their domain, blah blah blah."

"Okay, neat, but I still hope I'm not the only person you called!" Miles shouted.

As if on cue, a small fighter craft strafed the urban battlefield, and dropped what looked to be a person from its bomb bay doors as it swooped low to the ground. None other than the Redarian Jarrek Wöllschlager, charging the Voidspawns with a Claymore about as tall as himself while shouting battlecries that mostly amounted to warnings that his foes were utterly doomed.

Miles used the opportunity to then move in on the Voidspawns now distracted by Jarrek's display, and just before he was about to cut one of them down, a bolt of The Aura blasted its head off.

"I had him!" Miles shouted to Veralis, realizing full well who just robbed him.

Another Voidspawn crashed through the wall of a nearby building, soon disintegrating in its death throes. Miles peered in and saw Micah dealing with a few others alongside Miirkae. Dorg was yet to be found, but Miles was sure he'd be around somewhere.

The fight continued, and Miles found himself in a hell of a rhythm, moving from Voidspawn to Voidspawn, not in a battle trance of sorts, because a trance dulls the senses. He was more in an 'engaged' state, moving from foe to foe, as was everyone else around him. Dorg eventually was found, tossing his void-born opponents like sandbags into walls, rubble, sharp debris, everywhere. Dorg appeared to be a rather throw-heavy guy. With everyone working as a team, the city was soon cleared of the Voidspawns. Apparently, the rift had already been dealt with, and clean-up was all that was left. In the aftermath, Arakai found Miles in a ruined bar.

"I thought you might be in one of these, and I especially thought you'd seek out being alone," Arakai commented.

"Well, it's not *vital* that I'm alone. More just that a lot of these are perishable and will go bad before anyone starts rebuilding here, so I don't want 'em to go to waste." Miles said, tossing an empty bottle aside. It was at this moment Arakai noticed that was his fourth bottle of Lysanarr Semi-Spirit. About as strong as a light beer, but doesn't keep too well outside of a fridge. Easy to drink a lot of.

Arakai grabbed a few bottles and set them on the

counter for the two of them, complimenting Miles's skill. "You fight well, and have definitely improved since Hulae."

Miles was initially confused, then Arakai clarified that he saw some of the footage that was recovered from the city. Even after that, Miles still was surprised at the compliment. "Thanks... I don't think I've ever heard that before."

"I can't say I'm surprised. But you've earned that one."

Once again, Miles was shocked, and he looked it, checking the bottle he was on to make sure it was the drink he thought it was.

"Never heard that one either?" Arakai asked, and Miles nodded. "Hell, no wonder Veralis has been frustrated lately."

This confused Miles most of all, but he figured he wasn't nearly done being confused, and wouldn't be for a while. "What? How in all the realms would that frustrate Veralis?"

"Radien, she's a Psionic Empath, and has been since even before she was an Aura Warrior. She's highly intuitive, too. Normally she doesn't even need that power of hers to know what's generally going on in someone's head. But you... she can't get anything from you. And it's not just that, it's *why* she can't glean anything. She told me that... the way your mind is locked, it's far too potently impossible to get a feel for to be natural. It's trained. And not just casually, either. She's convinced that at some point, you must have deliberately chosen to spend multiple years consciously working and training to have your mind encased in a fortress, multiple fortresses even. She told me she's never seen walls so thick and expertly crafted."

"Try decades, Arakai. Over two whole ones," Miles commented, sipping his drink. "Is that a crime? It was absolutely necessary, and if I didn't teach myself such vigilance and analytical ability, if I didn't study every which way to discern ulterior motives, I would not be sitting here right now. I'd be dead a dozen times over."

"And *that's* what frustrates her. Not the fact that you did, but the fact that you *had to*. Neither she nor I, or Micah, Jarrek, Dorg or Miirkae doubt the necessity of your walls, nor do I personally want to criticize their craftsmanship. The strongest walls require the most skilled artisans to erect them."

"Arakai, you do realize what this sounds like to me, right?" Miles pointed out. "It sounds like someone trying to worm their way in. And granted, I don't think you're the kind of person to do that. I really don't. But I hope you understand why this sounds suspicious."

"I'll bet it is!" Arakai agreed. "I mean, it's a lot

<FIRE TO BURN THE STARS>

easier to walk through a gate than bust down a wall!"

Miles turned his head slightly in further confusion. "Your honesty is out of pattern, to be sure. I don't think any Human would actually be willing to even acknowledge that sort of thing."

"Is it any wonder why you prefer the company of non-humans?" Arakai said, raising a fresh bottle.

"Not in the slightest." The two clinked their bottles together and finished their drinks. They then heard a crash. Micah was practicing diving out windows and landing dramatically, with Jarrek critiquing. Miles got up, and Arakai assured that he'd continue working on the stash of drink.

Micah's approach to the dramatic landing was essentially to roll out of the fall and stand up with an upward slash, a rather practical version, to Miles's approval.

"I'm just glad it's not that ridiculous all-on-the-knee landing," Miles said, and Jarrek nodded. Micah still seemed slightly unsatisfied with her overall execution. But in time, she'd likely have a signature dramatic landing of her own.

The levity was cut short, however, as a final Voidspawn lurched towards them. But they should've been able to sense it approaching, their passive psionic instincts should've tipped them off. The Voidspawn was

<GREGOR FJELLREV>

clearly injured, however, and not long for this world.

The Voidspawn lifted its hand up and pointed at Miles. Even though it was hard to tell if it had fingers, the intent was clear. It was pointing at him.

"When will it be?" it said in its raspy, otherworldly voice. "How long until it burns?"

The Voidspawn collapsed, falling apart into nothingness.

"The hell'd he mean by that?" Miles asked coldly.

"Moreover, why didn't we know he was coming?" Veralis cut in. "If there's a new breed of Voidspawn that can exist beyond the inherent instinct of power-wielders, then the universe is in trouble."

"It didn't die like a typical Voidspawn," Jarrek commented. "The way that it seemed to be in a state of flux... as its form was being sheared and split..."

"Are we gonna just glaze right over the fact that he basically pointed at me and went to full Ominous Prophecy Mode?" Miles noted.

"I haven't forgotten," Micah said. "Even if it doesn't all add up, none of it bodes well. This might not have even been a Voidspawn, for all we know, but something else entirely."

"I'd be willing to bet that this thing just wanted to make a final intimidation roll, as it were," Veralis quickly assured. "The Voidspawns are willing to try just about anything. We should move out soon, let everyone know that rebuilding can get underway."

Veralis's insistence on the benign nature of this occurrence troubled Miles. As everyone was returning to their ships, Miles stopped Jarrek at his.

"Those glasses record?" Miles asked. Jarrek nodded. "Send me the footage of that thing." He nodded again, and Miles started heading towards a different city on Homphalion, he had been meaning to spend some time on this planet for a while.

The rest of the day was spent recreating, and Miles even landed a gig performing at the town square park in this place near to Reynvol, called Klunn. The original performing group had backed out for unknown reasons, but Miles said that if there was a replicator, he could do it, and the Hajivakk were happy to take the miracle.

Something that Miles had been doing lately with his guitar playing had been 'programming' songs to his Autotelekinetic Cantrips, so that he could play a song correctly without even having to think about it, which made vocals a hell of a lot easier. It was definitely an ability he had fantasized about back on Earth, being able to not have to worry about messing up a note here or a word there.

With the Haji-Son's favorite form of poetry being

'Non-Contextual Soliloquy,' the best kinds of songs to play were historical ballads, and even if they didn't know exactly what the specific names meant, they clearly could feel the message. Non-Contextual Soliloquy, of course, is the art of writing dramatic speeches minus the story they would go in, seeing as many times, one might have to write an entire story around working that speech in. And quite honestly, it would show.

Upon returning home, Miles noticed that Jarrek had sent him the recording of the being that approached them with its cryptic words back in Reynvol. So he took his ship to Turazin, and asked Xenidar for a private terminal. Uploading the footage of the creature, The Hideout searched for its identity. While the search ran, Miles summoned the Effigy again.

"What disturbs me about this is the fact that Veralis didn't postulate that the thing and its words were benign, she *assured* it. Almost on the level of insistence. She knows something about that creature that I don't, and if she was so quick to not tell me, then it means that she does not intend to."

The Effigy sat on a nearby chair as Miles sighed, resting his elbows on the desk and his chin in his hands. "What the hell could that thing be that Veralis wouldn't want me knowing? It's not like her to be like that, to withhold what's likely vital information..."

<FIRE TO BURN THE STARS>

The Hideout's computer completed its search, but returned an error: *INFORMATION ACCESS UNAVAILABLE, PROTOCOL BH-2980.*

"I'm sorry, what?" Miles asked, now more confused than ever.

The door opened behind him, and Xenidar switched off the terminal. "Follow me. I wouldn't do this for anyone else."

The two stepped into an elevator, and Xenidar gave it a voice command. "Core Archive, Sector Raven-9, authorization: Xenidar Ralkas, Hideout Leader, plus one."

The elevator began its descent towards the core of Turazin, where the most guarded relics of information were, along with the Geothermal Engine that powered a fair amount of the Hideout's systems. Not all of them, but most.

"I wouldn't do this for any other circumstance, either," Xenidar stated. "But the fact of the matter is that you deserve to know if you want to. But that said, you can still back out of that."

"Why would I do that? The worst it could tell me is that I'm about to die."

"Fair enough, never thought of it like that." Xenidar then cleared his throat. "The Black Records are everything that is stored on paper. It's never transcribed, never electronically translated into new languages, nothing that so much as beeps lays an eye on it. Computers can be hacked, even The Hideout's, given enough time. But you cannot hack paper."

"And I assume that every scrap of it in those records is that way for a very good reason?"

Xenidar nodded. "Some information is just too damn volatile to trust anyone with. More often than not, it's locations. Locations of this proto-civilization, or that ancient planet. Too many people would want the pride of controlling the special place, as it were.

Miles sighed. "This is why one of my old acquaintances on Earth said that Jerusalem should be bulldozed and paved. So that nobody gets to have the special place."

"It's not a uniquely Human trait."

The elevator stopped, and the two passed through a field that looked for any electronics on them, and Miles removed the comm-link from his pocket to place it in the elevator's lead-lined side compartment, per Xenidar's instruction. A five-mile walk followed to what looked to be a solid wall. Xenidar motioned for Miles to look away, and after he did, input a code into a hidden panel, and then a small rod extended from the wall. Xenidar concentrated for a moment, and the rod retracted. It must've been some kind of Psionic biometric scanner. Psionometric? That was likely the term.

Hydraulics then pulled the wall back, and moved it to the side, allowing the two entry into the Black Records. The wall moved back into its place soon after, and the glow of florescent light bulbs were all that lit the rooms.

"The primitiveness is necessary," Xenidar said, and Miles nodded. "Wait here."

The Talvas Vulpian then searched for a file cabinet, opened it up, and grabbed a folder from it, before placing it on the metal table that, along with the cabinets and lights, were the only furniture in the room. The file read "Time Enders"

Miles opened the file, and read.

These entities are likely as old, if not older than sentient life in the universe. Attempts to actively seek out these beings have all failed, as they appear to exist exclusively at-will. Records of the Time Enders are scattered and completely without pattern or consistency, the earliest depiction from the Third Cosmic Era, shortly before the First War for Reality.

A photograph depicted a black stone wheel dotted with red pictographs, runes and gems, the caption reading "Artifact identified as 'The Dread Wheel'"

The Dread Wheel shows an ancient civilization, presumably the one its artisan belonged to, encountering the being that they simply called The Ender, who pointed at a single individual, and stated 'The innocence of time wanes' before collapsing into nothingness. The Dread Wheel was created a few months later by the individual The Ender spoke its words to. Less than 20 Average Solar Cycles (ASC) later, the First War for Reality began. The archaeological team that unearthed the Dread Wheel noted an overwhelming sense of existential despair whenever they were within eyeshot of the artifact. Photograph was taken shortly before another member of the team destroyed it in a fit of delirium.

Reports of Time Enders are scattered and very seldom confirmed, but the most substantial confirmed sighting of a Time Ender took place in the Sixth Cosmic Era, which grants effective pseudo-confirmation of other sightings, as they all hold the same pattern: The Time Ender points at a single individual, and states a cryptic and ominous sentence, before disintegrating. What happens to the individual varies in case to case, but it always results in "A terrible realization, that often leads to taking one's own life" within the period of five Average Solar Days (ASD).

"This is the creature," Miles then said, looking at some surprisingly detailed artwork of the Time Ender mentioned in the Sixth Cosmic Era report. "This is what was on Reynvol."

Xenidar nodded. "When you uploaded Jarrek's

footage to the search terminal, I managed to isolate it and put it on a data drive that I'll be adding to the file, along with his inevitable written report of the incident"

"But I still don't know why Veralis was so quick to dismiss that thing. How the hell would she know what it was?"

"Finish reading that, Radien."

Miles looked at the final note on the page, and said five words in quiet horror.

Individuals singled out by a Time Ender sometimes report knowing exactly what the creature is, and in some cases, the meaning of their words.

"It wasn't pointing at me."

After returning to Cynofrax, Veralis was in the Holographic arena, tossing a rubber ball at one of the walls over and over again, catching it as it rebounded each time.

"Ask me in five days," Veralis said before Miles started, and he nodded, heading over to his Pondering Room, and summoning the Effigy once more.

"The part that makes the least sense is my investment in this," Miles pondered aloud. "Anyone else, and I couldn't care less. But not only do I find myself caring, I find myself realizing that it's not just Veralis I'd do this for. Arakai, Micah, Jarrek... every non-Human who has ever been a friend to me, I'd be doing this for them

<GREGOR FJELLREV>

too, if it were them it applied to."

Miles downed the drink he had for himself and the Effigy almost looked concerned. No, not concerned, not quite. If concern could come without its emotional traits, and be just the raw phenomenon of observing something unfortunate yet true, this was it. Just a strange kind of understanding that this is here, and that it has to be gotten through.

"It doesn't make sense. It's not how I work. Well, it's not how I work for Humans... Even so, it still feels off and unlike me. I must approach this with caution, and vigilance as always. I'd rather figure this out right than quick."

They both nodded, and Miles dismissed the Effigy.

After downing the drink he had for the Effigy, Miles stood up and stretched. "All right, what now?"

As soon as he exited the room, He saw a padded stick was thrown at him. He caught it in his left hand as Veralis exclaimed, "Defend yourself!"

Miles quickly and enthusiastically parried the first few of Veralis's strikes, eager to train in this drill. The two went at it for a bit, before Miles trapped her weapon arm, and when she tried to jab with her off hand, Miles grabbed that, and pulled it forward, soon having her arms crossing each other, and then used it as a fulcrum to throw her onto the ground. Veralis was undeterred overall, and kicked at Miles's shin with a straight side kick, throwing the leg out. Even though Miles didn't fall, and quickly regained his balance, Veralis had enough time to stand back up and reset the fight. The two stood there for a bit, before backing off.

"That was a cool throw," Veralis commented.

"I've always wanted to see if it really worked," Miles replied. "It's... so nice to be able to have a sparring partner to test stuff with. I've said that a lot before though. You're probably tired of it."

"That doesn't stop it from being true. It is wonderful to be able to just do that. Spar and test stuff."

Not long later, Miles got curious about how the Conclave was handling things on Earth. He knew he was so far from being a rare case in wanting to leave, and felt compelled to head over to the Conclave's stations there to see if they were really evacuating Humans, or just cherrypicking.

"I think honestly, a lot of people will be comforted by you visiting here, Radien," one of the administrators said as he led Miles into a meeting room with a map of the Earth. "Some people who definitely want to leave are hesitant to get in touch with us because they think it's just another trick or something."

"I know I would at first. Too good to be true," Miles said, and the Woran Cos administrator stopped in place, then pointed to him in the kind of gesture to mean he hit the nail right on the head. The Woran Cos were a cousin species to the late Kendrosians, an avian sort with very potent inherent Psionic proficiency.

"But yeah, we're really working at it here," he continued, bringing up a holographic globe, with about 20 ships orbiting the planet. "We have eyes over the entire surface with this, and anyone can signal that they want out. Techs are working around the clock, looking for 'em. A transmitted message, a mirror signal, hell, we've gotten a fair amount of people who were just waving their arms in the air and shouting. We dispatch a craft, and get them on board one of these colony-grade cruisers, give 'em quarters until the process is figured out, and medical attention if needed. We assess their skills, their morals, and make a choice from there. None of the final decisions are done with automation or algorithms."

"And what happens to the ones you reject?" Miles said with a hint of concern.

"The kind of people who get rejected don't even necessarily want to try to leave in the first place, and the few that we have sent back were either trying to infiltrate the colony, as it were, tried to buy their way out with the kind of personal wealth outright illegal on some planets, or genuinely thought we'd be just as shitty as them."

A moment passed, with Miles not entirely convinced.

"Look, if you want, I can pull up the list of rejects, and the specific reasons why."

Miles nodded, and the list popped up, names and faces. A fair amount of them were listed as "INFILTRATION ATTEMPT, GENERAL," with a few attached images for proof, most of them showing red armbands in desk stashes, a swastika flag adorning a home wall, regalia of other hate groups, a black and white version of the American flag with a single blue stripe. and speaking of the Americans, many of the reject's proof images showed confederate flags hanging from the front of their homes. Miles laughed.

"This makes me feel a hell of a lot better, yes. Thanks, man."

"I know I said it already, but I get it," the biped owl commented. "New species are being recognized by the Conclave all the time. Some are shoo-ins, others are questionable. Did you know that before their extinction, the Elurians were almost exactly like this?"

Miles shook his head. "All I've heard of the Elurians was that they were one of the biggest contributors to Psionic Studies in history."

"They *became* one of the biggest contributors to Psionic Studies in history. The Elurians were at the forefront of the 'de-stylization' of wielding Cosmic Power. The sort of... realization that there wasn't 'one more powerful than all the others,' or even that much of a ranking to it at all, that it's all on the wielder and how they use it."

Miles's curiosity was piqued.

"Before that, getting them into the wider universe looked pretty similar to what's happening down below right now. And I already kinda know your questions. What if the ships hit capacity? We'll get another one over here with all haste. Even then, twenty of these things can fit about one and a half times the Human population of the planet. Supplies? Yes. Cost? No. There were a fair number of Elurians just like you who had those concerns, who had an overall disdain and lack of faith for their species, who got the ball rolling on great things to come."

"Thanks," Miles said. "It's still really odd to be hearing stuff like that from anyone else."

"And I'll bet you'd never believe it from one of your kind. The Elurians back then wouldn't have."

Miles could only nod in agreement. His endorsement of the process the Conclave was utilizing resulted in a spike in the amount of Humans looking to leave Earth, and all of the ones who suddenly revealed themselves were eventually allowed to relocate, though it did take a bit of reassurance that Fortem Terra Nova was not the only option. Some seemed to be under that impression with the 'same shit, different pile' analogy being prevalent. It soon became the case that Humans heading to Fortem Terra Nova were in the minority.

At his home, Miles pondered again about entirely different things.

"The last mystery of old, what is that word?" The Effigy soon appeared to sit across from him.

"I've been looking for it for years. None of the ones in my language ever worked for it. Never did it justice, they all seemed so plain, so shallow..."

Miles didn't look confused, but more a hybrid of concentrating and tired. "What goes beyond just being an ally or friend. The ultimate ally, as it were. But that's not the world, 'ultimate ally.' Because it seems to go beyond definition. It transcends into understanding. You hear that word and you just *know* what that means..."

He hung his head down a bit, staring into the amber drink he had in front of him.

"Even if never what it feels like, or who that would be. But that does not despair me." He picked his head back up, and stood straight. "No, I cannot let it become a bad thing. Hating the fact that I stand alone does not change it. Why then do I ponder this word?"

The effigy also seemed to be both confused and

concentrating. It was giving him a run for his money too.

"It's not how I work, dammit! That's not how I operate!" He slammed his fist on the table in frustration that this conflict even existed. The Effigy wasn't startled. "I am steel and I am doom! I cannot, I *must* not be swayed by just one truth! I didn't train myself as well as I did just to be destroyed by one measly fact! That's not what gets to kill me! It's not what gets to be my undoing!"

Miles sat back down, took a breath, then a drink. "I'll be fine. I've been able to be for this long, and since things are getting better, It'll only be easier. I'm just glad no one has to be around for me to sort this out, and they can see what they should of me."

Miles sighed one last time before his final comment. "Radien stands alone, but that is my strength." He then dismissed the Effigy.

Not long after, Veralis arrived at the house, carrying a box to the workshop, snickering. Miles decided to head over to the city of Alindros itself to find somewhere to play some guitar. He had been working on a song enhanced by use of The Aura's Autotelekinetic Cantrips so that he could play complex guitar riffs whilst singing, and not lose concentration on either. In one of the public parks that allowed music exhibition, he set himself up, and began with a base rhythm of power chords that the amp soon was playing on a loop for him to improvise over, and soon the lyrics started.

I will bring the fire, and I will bring the flood
I will forge the steel, and I will hew the stone
I will fight all my foes unto the end of time
And thus, I am Doom!
A search that cannot begin,
matters not when it is over
I remain the fortress and the obelisk
And even if the skies don't clear,
I will be the one to split them
I will not allow myself to face defeat!
I will bring the fire, and I will bring the flood
I will forge the steel, and I will hew the stone
I will fight all my foes unto the end of time
And thus, I am Doom!
My foes tremble before me, and they are right to so
For my will is as the mountain and the citadel
A tempest of my power, a storm to shatter heavens
And the drive to be a better man as warrior!
I will bring the fire, and I will bring the flood
I will forge the steel, and I will hew the stone
I will fight all my foes unto the end of time
And thus, I am Doom!

As he played the solo that bridged the second chorus and third, he only then looked up and noticed the

<GREGOR FJELLREV>

crowd he had drawn, they were enjoying what he was playing, and clearly mosh pits weren't exclusively a human phenomenon.

> *I will bring the fire, and I will bring the flood*
> *I will forge the steel, and I will hew the stone*
> *I will fight all my foes unto the end of time*
> *And thus, I am Doom!*

At the end of the closing riff, the crowd was cheering. It was the biggest audience he'd ever had, and they wanted to hear more. Miles of course, obliged with a few songs from Sabaton and Rhapsody of Fire with the same general feel as his opener.

Something told him he'd not be paying for his own drinks for the next few days in Alindros. That little performance of his, and the revelry after was certainly a good stress reliever, and started heading back home to debrief before Arakai grabbed his attention.

"Radien! Glad I caught you here." It seemed as though Arakai had been in the crowd. "Hell of a show!"

"Thanks, Arakai. What'd you need?"

"What? Nothing! I wanted to invite you over to my place after that, we definitely need to put something together!"

"Oh... Well, in that case, that sounds good! Lead the way."

Arakai's place was about the size of the average

apartment in a highway town between major cities. Meaning that it could comfortably fit three relatively low-maintenance individuals for about the price of a 1 bedroom city apartment, but it wasn't rented, considering the condominium nature of the building.

"It might not be much, but I think it works," Arakai commented.

"Nah, I think it works too," Miles said.

Arakai's instrument appeared to be a sort of 'precision guitar' that collectively could play about as many notes as a grand piano, but the frets were more compressed together, and the strings precision-engineered from Kittorik Metal, a hybrid of the silk of Trylaxian Skyspiders and Tungsten, which resulted in an extremely durable, extremely strong material to serve as the strings for a very precisely made instrument.

After several hours of brainstorming and practice, there followed some sparring since they hadn't fought each other yet, and wanted to get that squared away. Arakai was able to force Miles to tap out in the first bout, since he was more accustomed to ground fighting than Miles, but retribution was swift, and Arakai found himself having to yield to Miles's unrelenting striking. After an exchange of pointers, the two had a drink together.

"I've honestly been thinking about what you said at first," Arakai started. "When you asked what I needed."

Miles chuckled. "Does it say that much of what I've come to expect people to think of me?"

"Not necessarily. But I'd bet you could call yourself treated like a god in the manner of 'Existence unacknowledged until someone needed a personal favor?'

Miles scoffed and thudded his head on the table. "Ouch. Called right the hell out. That's my job normally."

Arakai held back his next comment, but Miles insisted on not having things sugarcoated for him. "All right, then. I was gonna postulate next that you've been conflicted lately because everyone's being the one who listens to you, when normally that's what you do? And as a result, you wonder if you're becoming just another fool who talks?"

"I think what comforts me is that I don't actually do *that* kind of talking. I'm not telling you all my problems and my tribulations. What does make me uneasy is how many people are saying that I can talk to them. If I had a twig for every time someone told me that, their voice dripping with the fact that they didn't *really* mean it, I could build a fire to torch a moon planetside."

Miles's voice switched to an almost tired tone. "People never wanted to help. They wanted to say that they could, and be able to take credit when you managed to figure it out yourself. 'See that guy over there who got through that part of his life? I was there for him.' That's what people wanted to do."

"I'll bet you've heard it a lot already, but that's *Humans* that want that," Arakai assured.

"I've heard it most of all from myself in reminder. Maybe someday I'll listen properly." Miles then drank the rest of his glass. Arakai simply nodded his head in a way to suggest he was already doing that, in a way.

After that day at Arakai's, Miles started heading back to his home. On the way, however, something felt off. The Aura seemed to be tipping him off that something was up, and the shop he was passing was at the center of it. It was a specialty tech store, offering commission work for computers and hobby-level tools. Miles walked in, and realized what The Aura was on about. There was a group of five Humans in the store, idling about in a perfectly nonchalant manner that basically meant there was no way they actually planned to buy anything. Miles looked over to the male Vulpian behind the counter, who shrugged his shoulders slightly. Seems both of them were getting hairs standing on end.

A quick check with The Sight later, and Miles saw the weapons three of them were carrying. Wait, there were four weapons. One of them was just... right behind him?

<GREGOR FJELLREV>

If it weren't for The Aura, Miles would've been knocked out cold by the wooden buttstock of a smuggled shotgun from Earth to the back of his head as its wielder shouted for everyone to get down. Miles whipped around, grabbing his assailant by the throat, and slamming her headfirst onto the floor with a yell. In pure rage, he began stomping on her throat. He hated this Human for trying to hit him while his back was turned. He hated her far more than he had hated anyone else he'd ever seen in his life today. There was no coldness to his actions, just seething brutality as he cursed and crushed the coward's throat and head with his boot. Miles then turned his sight on the other armed robbers, who until then had been standing there in shock. Miles charged at the first, who wasn't able to raise his weapon in time before Miles grabbed him and put his body in front of the other two as they emptied their guns into their friend. With the aid of The Aura, Miles immediately then slammed his body into the one on the left, catapulting him into the wall. The last guy couldn't reload fast enough, and Miles grabbed his arm and yanked him into his extended fist, rocking his head back hard enough to break a few vertebrae in his spine.

There were only two now alive. One who was still dazed from his trip into the wall, and the last who hadn't even gotten the chance to fight yet, and was now trying to run. Miles threw a knife at his leg, and it stuck, thanks to the Equilibrium Autotelekinetic Cantrip Miles had worked on. He then grabbed the man he slammed into the wall, and threw him outside with his comrade. He was barely able to muster the coordination to pull a knife from his belt and stab at Miles, which only earned him a broken arm. The last one, still trying to run, soon had that knife embedded in his other leg. Both of them tried to plead for their lives, but Miles was having none of it. Maybe if they hadn't brought weapons. Maybe if one of them hadn't tried to hit him in the back of the head. But right now, mercy was not an option.

"You have lost your right to surrender by trying to beat me like a fucking coward!" Miles shouted, tearing out the throat of the one he was still holding on to, then walked over towards the last one, who could only crawl now.

"You thought you were fucking invincible, didn't you?!" Miles yelled, conjuring energy in his fist. "You woke up today with the thought in your head that you were gonna be shitty, and get away with it! You thought with your stupid fucking guns and your cowardly way of non-fighting that you could get a quick score?!"

A Planetary Guardsman suddenly ran between them and held his shield in front of Miles as another picked the heavily wounded Human up, intending to take him away. "It's over now, stand down!" the Guardsman said, his free hand extended behind his body as a signal of yielding.

"That coward still fucking lives!" Miles shouted. The Guardsman then looked over to the shop, and saw the mangled other four.

"You got four of them!" he then insisted. "Four out of five, and you've definitely scared him into never wanting to even look at a—"

Miles took the chance to fire that bolt through the head of the Human, about to be out of his hands. The body went limp, a charred hole where a brain used to be. The Planetary Guardsman holding him had dove out of the way, even though he wasn't going to be hit, and the other hit the deck as Miles warped out as quickly as he realized both what he had just done, and what that might mean for him.

The next three days he spent on Zharekk, at Xatrial Isenhart's fortress. After he had recovered the Manifest of Apocalypse, Moldrenor and his crew packed up from there since there was nothing more needed at the time. As for Miles asking if he could have the fortress, Moldrenor at the time had basically said, "I don't know, can you?" Which proved useful, as Miles had now essentially exiled himself there.

Near the morning of day four, Miles heard one of

the landmines blow up outside, followed by minor cursing. Miles shot up, alert and ready for battle, looking toward the roof panel that would inevitably be accessed. But when it opened up, a familiar Zharekai Vulpian descended down, though Miles kept a safe distance with his guard up.

"I wondered if you'd be here," Moldrenor said.

"And how are things out in the universe?" Miles asked, leaning against a wall.

"Things are fine."

"Do not lie to me."

Moldrenor sighed. "The Humans on Fortem Terra Nova are in an uproar. They've basically been calling you 'A dangerously powerful and enhanced individual' and are simultaneously scared and envious of your ability to wield Cosmic Power."

"And they've proposed my execution?" Miles scoffed.

"No, but I'd bet they'd like to." Moldrenor chuckled. "You've exiled yourself here, and Cynofrax's parliament is recognizing that as your punishment. Of course, the Humans don't like it, since of course they don't, and it's already looking like war will be happening. War that will result in the extinction of the Human race, and rather handily, and over five of theirs that already had bounties on them."

Miles leaned against a wall as Moldrenor continued. "The Conclave ships have pulled out of Earth, and both Human planets are gearing up. Already a few spies have been snatched on Redaria Omega and Teyn-Var-Wolk."

"So what happens afterwards? When the Humans are quickly wiped from the universe?"

"Well, then the Conclave basically says that since everyone who was complaining is now gone, there's no reason for you to be in exile. In truth, you could leave at any time to fight the Humans, since the result is the same in the end."

"But I can't imagine my friends are happy about it." Miles knew there had to be a catch somewhere.

"Does it matter? Friends come and go, alliances reveal their shaky grounds, and new ones are sought. That's how it's worked, isn't it?"

Miles now was confused and slightly concerned. "True, but... that was for Humans. I honestly thought I had something going for me here, with the friends I already had made. And if I know my friends like I might know myself... they won't be proud of me, more likely ashamed that this is how it went."

Miles then sat down at the wall he was leaning on. "They... had hope for me. No one had ever done that before, not truly like them. And I failed that hope, that faith they put in me. And the worst part is that I still don't regret what I did."

"And this is where it burns," Moldrenor suddenly said. Radien stood up, alarmed, and watched as Moldrenor fell apart like the Time Ender did back on Homphalion. Suddenly, the fortress crumbled around him, and the ruins gave way to the cityscape of Reynvol, just after the battle. Miles then fell to his knees, exhausted, and looked around him. The others hadn't finished checking for stragglers yet. Miles scrambled over to where the Time Ender was, and scan-pulsed the ground, that now had a metallic sheen across it that was rapidly fading, as if someone had poured bismuth over the rocks, and the rocks were absorbing it.

Sure enough, he was able to catch the trace there and log it. He then fell back to a sitting position and breathed heavily. Jarrek was soon there, asking what the hell just happened.

"You ever heard of a Time Ender?" Miles asked.

"By the gods..." Jarrek simply responded. Clearly he had some idea of what Miles just went through. He then grabbed the scanner and looked at the readings, nodding.

Miles soon went over to The Hideout to deliver his account of the Time Ender to Xenidar, who looked at it, then to Miles again.

"The thing about the readings you got..." Xenidar said. "They're the first solid, material evidence recorded of the Time Enders, which effectively just graduated them out of myth. There's gonna be a lot of study into these, but I can tell right off the bat from 'em that you really did experience those days, and those events. When it first pointed at you, it created a sort of chrono-anchor on that exact moment, to loop you back to once it was finished."

"So there really are Black Records, then?"

"It's not exactly a secret that they exist, but I don't complain about the lack of knowledge that they do."

At the very least, Miles had a new song out of the ordeal, which he decided he'd play in Sorrenikas, just to be safe. When he headed to the store at the time the robbery took place last time, it never actually happened, much to his relief. There weren't even any Human visitors that whole day.

When he finally got home for the first time in what seemed like forever, he summoned the Effigy once again.

"Does the time that I talked to you in the time-slip count?"

The Effigy nodded. An uncommon occasion, but not once in a lifetime.

"Good. I'm not fond of repeating myself. But that Time Ender... what was the point of him?"

ACT V
IN THE SHADOW
OF EXEMPLARS

Kendro-Dalinor? And you're sure he wanted to see me?"

Miles had just been told that a message was waiting from him from the Haji-Son Exemplar by that name. He wasn't quick to believe that after one small favor, Kendro-Dalinor would already have Miles on his contact list.

"Aye." The Hajivakk messenger nodded.

"Any reason he couldn't have just called me?"

"He doesn't have your number."

"Okay, fair enough," Miles noted, then headed towards the Aura Runner to warp to Caren'Das, and meet with the Exemplar.

When Miles eventually met with Kendro-Dalinor again, he could tell that something was off about him. As much as Miles wasn't a people person, let alone one who could easily tell when someone was having internal conflict, Kendro-Dalinor looked with the kind of unnerve that might affect someone who just learned the date and time of their death.

"So, what's this about?" Miles asked. "All I've really done for you so far is get that information ark from Alabasteron, I don't think it exactly makes me a trusted confidant."

"Your work on Alabasteron, however, does tell me that you could be. With how you handled yourself there, it tells me that you're the closest thing to the most trustworthy person on this matter."

Miles stood there, not more concerned as much as more unsure what might make the Haji-Son Exemplar act like this. "So what makes this a matter I have to be party to?"

"It is... exceptionally difficult to explain, and I'm not sure if there's enough hours left in the day to do it. But I am not about to ask you to do something beyond your moral code, that I can promise. If it weren't for the demands of my office as Exemplar, I'd go acquire this item myself."

Kendro-Dalinor then projected a hologram of a cylindrical device on his desk, about the size of the average wine bottle, made of some kind of stone.

"It is an artifact known as the Cey-Tavn Shroud," he explained, and Miles raised an eyebrow. "Archaeotech like this have been known to have incredible abilities, that haven't been able to be replicated since the Third and Fourth Cosmic Eras."

"Like the Dread Wheel?" Miles asked.

"Yes, precisely like the Dread Wheel," Kendro-Dalinor agreed, surprised that Miles knew of that artifact. "In fact, the Cey-Tavn Shroud isn't too far in purpose from what the Dread Wheel was for. The idea was that it could hide someone from the forces of fate, particularly the kind that entails rotten luck."

"Sounds like something I could've used on Earth." Miles scoffed, then thought for a moment. "If it weren't for that fact, I might be hesitant to help you find a good luck charm. But I gather this more like an 'anti-bad luck' charm. I'll see what I can do, and out of my respect for you, Exemplar, I won't press on what makes you think you need this thing."

Kendro-Dalinor seemed a little confused as to why Miles felt the need to add the last part of that thought, and Miles could tell.

"I... eh, force of habit. Humans would normally press, and I know I would've been relieved whenever someone told me that they wouldn't. They never did, though..."

Kendro-Dalinor nodded understandingly, and Miles headed out. The trail started on Teyn-Var-Wolk, homeworld of the Woran Cos and the Nuvenr Draconians. Upon arriving, he met with Zalantrossos, a Woran Cos archaeologist Miles was told to contact in order to begin his search for the Cey-Tavn Shroud.

"Okay, now I remember, it was Owl," Miles muttered to himself as he tried to recall the closest Earth creature he knew the Woran Cos resembled.

"Do what now?" Zalantrossos asked.

"Oh, nothing, sorry," Miles stammered. "Exemplar Kendro-Dalinor said you're the person to ask about the Cey-Tavn Shroud."

Zalantrossos nodded, handing Miles a moderately sized book with highlighted passages. "The problem with finding named artifacts like this is that as they change hands, they often change names. It's entirely possible that something like the Eye of Akoraveon sitting in someone's coat pocket right now, and they're calling it the Talisman of Lor-Ragath for all I know." She sighed, then continued. "That's how you typically find archaeotech stuff like this. They're very rarely still sitting in dusty tombs and ruined vaults."

"The last known place of the Cey-Tavn Shroud, if this information is correct, was supposed to be here on Teyn-Var-Wolk."

"Emphasis on *supposed* to be," Zalantrossos gruffed. "It was being returned to this planet since it was made here by Woran Cos artificers, but the ship it was on, *Sanashaw's Message,* vanished en route, and wasn't heard from for a good fifteen ASC."

An ASC, or Average Solar Cycle, was equivalent to a little over three Earth years.

"That suggests that the location of *Sanashaw's Message* is known."

"Yup," Zalantrossos said, with a hint of annoyance. "The problem is that it's in the Bennet's Stand Field, and it's haunted."

Miles paused for a moment. "One problem at a time. Bennet's Stand Field?"

"At the end of the Artifactium Conflict in the Seventh Cosmic Era, everyone who had a bone to pick in that war agreed to bring all their militaries in all their ships to intergalactic space, lock it in a Graviton Field, and have it out. They voluntarily sterilized themselves so that they couldn't rear and raise children to fight the war for them, and banished themselves to it for however long they had left to live. The Graviton Field made sure neither they or the blown-up ships could leave. As such, no one's been able to escape if they found themselves trapped in it. But with modern teleport tech, that shouldn't be a problem these days."

Miles processed that for a second. "All right, but clearly *Sanashaw's Message* being in a gravity prison isn't the problem that is presented by being within the Bennet's Stand Field."

"Being a Graviton Field of its nature, ships within it sometimes find themselves coalescing and forming new lumps of metal that seem to still be fighting that war. Kinda like Alabasteron but in space."

"Must be," Miles said, remembering that he was the only living being knowing the truth of Alabasteron's skeletons. But he figured that lumps of metal had less of a sense of humor than multi-billion year old psionically immortal skeletons. "So Bennet's Stand still fights the Artifactium Conflict, but *Sanashaw's Message* is haunted on top of that?"

"For lack of a better word, yes," Zalantrossos hesitantly agreed. "It's honestly only really called *haunted* because no one's bothering to find out for sure."

Not long later, Miles and the Aura Runner were bound for the Bennet's Stand Field. It was the first time he'd actually been in the emptiness between galaxies. He was hesitant at first, and wondering if he should just let the ship run on autopilot with blinders over the cockpit itself.

"There's both no point in risking insanity and no

point in delaying what inevitably will have to be seen," Miles said to himself, as he neared the edge of the elliptical galaxy that Teyn-Var-Wolk called home. Warping from one to another seemed somehow less of a big deal for him than actually looking out at the raw distance itself. Perhaps it was because it all felt like the same area if one didn't have to actually see that distance before them.

The Aura Runner's lock on Bennet's Stand didn't falter as Miles could look back and see that he had crossed the threshold. As his ship flew further away, the view outside didn't actually look too far off from a typical night sky, the main difference being what those points of light were. But it inevitably still felt so surreal. He wasn't sure whether to be impressed or scared or gone mad. He was the first Human to see this sight, and though countless science fiction stories told tale of men who saw the void and lost their minds, the procedure for the real thing was yet unwritten.

It didn't sound any quieter than space within galaxies, yet it felt more silent, somehow. Miles pressed forth, and his ship eventually came within sight of the Graviton Field that surrounded Bennet's Stand.

"Probably about as far out as they could stand to get," Miles said to himself as he brought the ship to relative halt outside the field, and locked on to

Sanashaw's Message within. To his surprise, the vessel was still moving throughout the field, avoiding other clumps of debris. He then took a deep breath, and warped himself aboard with his personal Defense Grid Generator to make sure he could breathe.

As he suspected, the ship had no atmosphere, so the Oxygen Shield of the Defense Grid had to work its magic, even though The Aura could passively ensure his life. But Miles preferred it this way, however possible it was to not need it.

Moving throughout the ship, Miles found no remains. They likely would have decayed to dust by now anyway, even if he didn't actually know the UDM, or Universal Date Marker of the disappearance of the ship. Following his scanner, he looked for the Archaeotech signature.

His scanner led Miles to what looked like a coat locker. When he looked inside, it contained what appeared to be to be uniform jackets.

"Techbooth," Miles started. He had not long ago moved Techbooth to permanently reside within the Aura Runner as its computer. "Who were the Exiles of Karnous?"

"*The Exiles of Karnous, formerly the Honorable Order of the Men of Karnous, were an organization for war relief during the early Eighth Cosmic Era. They were*

<GREGOR FJELLREV>

formally disgraced by the Conclave of Sentience after it was discovered that they would often loot historical artifacts from former war zones with the cover of their work. This caused a split in the Order, as there were a significant number of members unaware of this ulterior motive. The Exiles of Karnous made it their express mission to return artifacts stolen by the Men of Karnous to their planets of origin. The Men of Karnous themselves eventually became a radical group promoting the philosophy of Kendradeyne's Folly, which teaches—"

"I got it," Miles cut off, and grabbed from the coat pocket of one jacket two nearly identical devices. One of them, the Cey-Tavn Shroud. The other, an elaborate replica.

"Wait..." Miles said, confused. "Why? Techbooth, can you access the crew's log at all?"

"The internal components of the ship are too degraded to extract the crew logs remotely. Access would only be possible from the physical hard drives."

"It won't be necessary," a voice said from behind Miles, and he whipped around with the AZP-621 pistol to see who just said that. A spectral form, appearing to be of the lost Kendrosian species. "I can just tell you."

"Well, they did say the ship was haunted," Miles recalled, holstering the weapon.

"And you seem quick to believe that, for a species

I've never seen before."

"By now I've spent more time out and about in this universe than on my home planet, and in that time I've fought and killed literal Demons, chatted with forest spirits, made many friends of many species, and spoken with the skeletons of Alabasteron. It'd be pretty silly to draw the line at ghosts."

"Neither of us are here to talk of worldliness," the Kendrosian spirit reminded.

"Correct. Do recount your story."

"After the denouncing of the Men of Karnous, we took *Sanashaw's Message*, along with many artifacts that the order had stolen, intending to return them to their owners, or the closest thing to them. Teyn-Var-Wolk was the last stop of this particular run, but one of our crewmen actually discerned the purpose of the Shroud. Many of the things the order took weren't artifacts of power, just trinkets from fallen empires or personal effects of the dead. The Cey-Tavn Shroud was the one thing we had that someone could properly think would be worth killing for."

"The most I heard of it was an anti-bad luck charm of sorts. Hide you from the hands of fate."

"True. But the thing is, that effect goes above and beyond what one might expect. Sure, you'll not have that fun event canceled, or you might not get sick this

Che'Vainen Flu season, but... it didn't make you lucky. What it did was to *eliminate* luck's absence to be able to make you lose. The wind suddenly died down before you were to fire a shot. Your number would happen to be drawn from the hat. Your enemy didn't notice you in the crowd. If it was a matter of luck, you couldn't *lose*. And wherever the situation was win or lose, no in between, well... there was only one outcome with the Shroud."

"And a crew of the size for this ship would be guaranteed to have at least one person who didn't really want to stop being one of the Men of Karnous..."

The Kendrosian spirit nodded. "I'd ask that you leave that here, or take it to the Defender. They've got a vault for artifacts like this. Things that are just too dangerous to be trusted in the hands of the universe. Things that only one person can hold, but should never be held by only one person..."

Miles then had a realization. "When did this ship become stranded out here?"

"Stranded? I diverted our warp course into Bennet's Stand because the Graviton Field would keep us locked in here until we sorted things! That... really didn't work out, though."

Miles looked at the spirit, still waiting for an answer.

"UDM 8-317,300,109-19-4..."

"A little under a hundred thousand ASC ago... three hundred thousand of my years."

"At least get the Shroud to my connections on Teyn-Var-Wolk! At least a few of them should still be around, even if their grandchildren."

"I... I don't think you realize... what's your name?"

"Pelivan."

"Pelivan, I wish I wasn't the one to have to tell you, but... Kendrosium fell. Caltoran was killed and corrupted, and your people... they're all gone. Eluria, too. I wasn't even born then, but I still somehow feel so much sorrow... For a people I never knew existed until eleven or twelve ASC ago, when I first left my home world."

At this point, Pelivan ceased his spectral hovering, and just stood on the ground, as if the weight of that knowledge was about to give his opaque body mass again.

"I don't understand... I almost feel on the verge of tears, but I was born after that... I... I surely do not have the right!"

Pelivan was silent and contemplative. "I did wonder why I never heard the drums of Kendra-Kai. They fell silent for me, and I felt an unfathomable dread like I knew a storm approached, and could do nothing."

Miles fell to his knees. "In my short time in this universe, I've heard the tales of Kendrosium, its proud and wise people! One of the oldest species in all the stars, destroyed by a Demon that puppeted who once was the protector!"

Pelivan sat against the wall, both men across from each other, sitting in apparent misery at events long ago.

"Where do we stand now, Pelivan?" Miles asked. "I've no right to feel pain for you. But your right is to some kind of final peace."

"The fact that there's still a universe for species to be introduced to means Caltoran fell eventually. At the cost of how many worlds, I shudder to think. But you didn't come here to weep about my people, or me. Yet... here we are."

"Oh, don't worry, Pelivan. I ran out of tears years ago. From them formed a bitterness that I still can't seem to get over."

Pelivan shook his head. "Physically, sure. But I can almost see the bawling in your mind, and the stones you angrily throw at the nearby trees. The shame that you feel for being sad on my behalf, and the conflict of whether or not its your place, because you'd rather help than commiserate."

"Well, obviously it's in my mind, can't go letting those things be done in the physical realm, where prying eyes can watch and ears listening for weakness can hear," Miles commented. "But that's not the only conflict. Look, this isn't how I work. And that's far from the first time I've warned myself that lately. I also hate the fact it likely won't be my last... But no, no. I can't be spilling my problems on to you, what must I do *now*, in this present day to bring you peace?"

"Whatever you do with the Shroud... it doesn't really concern me. It hasn't for quite a while. I've figured it's what's keeping me here, and if I can let go of that, it'll be good enough for me."

"No favor's too large, Pelivan. Not so long as I wield The Aura."

Pelivan chuckled slightly. "So you've been to Cynofrax, then? Met the Prism? You must be one of the good ones of your species. In that case..."

Pelivan suddenly stopped. He looked as though he had a favor to ask, only then realizing he no longer wanted it. "I... I was going to say 'win the war' or 'beat the Dark Six.' But that's a task countless have failed to do, including nine people that held the title of Universal Defender. I don't understand why, but I felt compelled to believe in you like I'd believe in Caltoran, or T'Sen before him. So tell you what: Prove me right to have felt that way. Find out what just made me believe in you, even though I don't know your name, and have never seen your species."

"My name is Miles Radien."

Pelivan suddenly perked, as if he just heard something he'd been waiting to hear for a very long time. "I can hear the drums..."

"Be at peace in Kendra-Kai, Pelivan."

The ghostly visage faded, and Miles was left with two cylindrical canister-like objects. "Okay, which one is which..." He said to himself, only then noticing that these were indeed canisters. Whatever was inside one of them was the Cey-Tavn Shroud.

Upon consulting Zalantrossos on Teyn-Var-Wolk, she agreed that the Shroud should not be in private hands, and when Kendro-Dalinor heard Miles's account of what the Shroud could do, he agreed, noting that the circumstance that made him desire possessing the artifact had passed without incident. With Zalantrossos's assurance that the Cey-Tavn Shroud would be kept safe in the city of Kandor's Museum of Archaeotech, Miles had finished Pelivan's mission of returning the artifact to the closest thing that existed to its owners.

"I am curious, Exemplar," Miles said during the debrief. "Would you be willing to tell me why you felt the need for the Shroud?"

"I recently came in contact with a rather particular Human who seemed to unnerve me with her very existence," Kendro-Dalinor said. "She has since left Caren'Das, however."

"Sometimes they're like that." Miles chuckled. "Did you get a name?"

"Amandrianna Sarvalimil."

Miles's froze, took a few deep breaths as he seemed to calm himself for battle at the sound of that name. "It's not you who would've needed the Shroud, Exemplar."

Zalantrossos's eyes narrowed. "You know this Human, Radien?"

"Long story. Kendro-Dalinor, keep your wits about you. I'll deal with Amandrianna in the meantime."

Miles hurried off towards The Aura runner and soon blasted off, leaving both Zalantrossos and Kendro-Dalinor in the dust, and exceptionally confused.

On Cynofrax, Veralis Stratenheim was studying a few classic Earth novels when her comm-link pinged. It was Exemplar Kendro-Dalinor.

"Exemplar. I don't recommend this book from Earth. It's just frustrating by concept. The title is awesome, it sounds badass. It sounds like a really thought-provoking, really poetic kind of book, but you open it and it's just... really disappointing and frustrating. It's Kendradeyne's Folly all over again," Veralis greeted.

"Which one is that?"

"It's called Atlas Shrugged. I feel so gods-damned betrayed." She then tossed the book across the room in mild frustration with an 'ugh, get outta here.'

"I'll make a note of that. But Veralis, did Radien ever mention a Human by the name of Amandrianna Sarvalimil?"

She thought for a moment, then informed Kendro-Dalinor that the name was unfamiliar.

"Apparently he just about went pale when I mentioned that she had been to Caren'Das, then blasted off in the Aura Runner. I had hoped you might have some insight."

"I don't, Exemplar. But if Radien is unnerved by the presence of a named Human, there's a damn good reason for it. I'll find out anything I can, and you may want to double your guard."

"I'll consider it a favor, and owe you one, Veralis."

Veralis knew that asking Miles was a slippery slope. The fact that she knew of the incident alone was one in and of itself, especially since Miles hadn't told her anything about it. Eventually, she concluded that Amandrianna Sarvalimil was an old enemy of Miles from Earth, and had managed to leave the planet either through illegal transport or lying through her teeth to the legal ones. The question of course, being where she would go after leaving Earth? The amount of Humans that were smuggling themselves off Earth wasn't large enough to really have a planet that they were prevalent on.

"Okay, if I were a foe of Radien, why would I find myself on Caren'Das?"

Then came to her realization. "Caren'Das is a major trade hub for the universe, being a pretty big planet with six moons. Not to mention the rest of that solar system has overall a hell of a lot of ground-space, more so than the average one. Naturally, information can easily be found there. Information like 'where is Miles Radien?'"

Veralis still had some friends within the networks of Caren'Das, both surface-level and underground. Running the name Amandrianna Sarvalimil didn't get a lot of answers, until one of her contacts replied.

"Amandrianna Sarvalimil has been forming connections in Caren'Das, mostly legal ones. The others are barely so, and it seems that was deliberate. She bartered by doing work patching up fight club members who took a few licks too many in exchange for travel records regarding none other than a one Miles Sorvenjar Radien, and enough money to get a space-worthy ship of her own." The Hajivakk contact Kia-Nahara explained. "She even asked if Miles had partaken in any of these clubs, so clearly she's trying to find him, but I'm not sure if she even fully understood why, if you ask me."

Veralis was able afterwards to convince Caren'Das's starports to put a watch on an Amandrianna

Sarvalimil. Not to stop her from leaving the planet, but to let Veralis know if and when she did, and where she was heading. Given that Amandrianna's only crimes thus far were aiding and abetting illegal combat sport participants, the planet's guardsmen wouldn't be able to do much in the way of searching for her, since there were higher-priority things to do than pursue someone who hadn't actually caused any proper damage yet.

However, after learning of the Aura Runner's presence on the nearby planet Mjarfus, in an area recently abandoned after multiple hurricanes, Veralis made a split-second decision to defy social convention and teleport directly over to the planet, a few miles outside of the flooded town. Cloaking herself with her own power, she made her way towards voices she was hearing, one of them clearly Miles.

"I'll never understand why you work the way you do," was Miles's first discernible sentence as Veralis listened. "There's just plain no need for you to be after me like this anymore."

"Why not?" came the response of who Veralis assumed was Amandrianna.

"Why not?! Why fucking not?! Because look around you! You're on a planet hundreds of thousands of light-years from Earth, under a sky you've never seen before! And just this solar system, it's got more planets that you could explore and live a life on than any of us could've imagined! And you still choose to be such as insufferable to *me alone* as you are?! I lived my whole fucking life on Earth under the boot of the anguish you loved to keep causing, and figures that you only start gunning for me again once I've not only found a better life for myself, and have actually got some accomplishments under my belt! My name will live on far longer than yours, and I dare to say that I'm happy now! Is that why you're here?!"

Whoever Amandrianna was to Miles, it certainly had a history of conflict at the friendliest times.

"I'm immortal now! I'm a wielder of the cosmic powers that be! I don't have to age if I don't want to, and I could rip your head off your neck with a wave of my hand! And I *delight* in how much I'll bet that burns you, how much you think *you* deserve it instead, how your pathetic sense of entitlement and elitism would have you say that I should've bent the knee to you again and always!"

Veralis thought to herself that Miles must've been waiting a long time to say that. For some reason, however, Amandrianna wore the smuggest shit-eating grin under this particular sun, leaning towards Miles, grinning ear to ear with her eyes almost closed like she had just won every argument in history.

Miles just laughed, soon hysterically. As the laugh wore down to just giggles and chuckles, he then fired a bolt into the air and created a massive explosion, and Amandrianna's smug smile faded as if only now did she realize that she could face consequences. "Now I can tell you that I'll never forget *that* look," Miles said. "Look at how scared you are that you can be held accountable. Remember always the fear you feel today, that you not only can be punished, but no one will be around to tell you that you were in the right. Now I cast the shadow, and your name won't even have the honor of infamy. Now turn around and run away! And pray to whatever gods you justify yourself with these days that our paths never cross again!"

Turn around and run away Amandrianna did, sprinting and fumbling through the flooded town, eventually disappearing into a transit tunnel as Miles just stood there, satisfied, shouting one last time "Run away!" as she did so, and firing another bolt of energy deliberately past her.

Veralis now had more questions than answers, so she quickly warped over into the ruined tunnel that Amandrianna was bound for, quickly giving one of the locals sitting against a wall a handful of currency to move from the spot and get himself some food.

Soon, Amandrianna was walking by Veralis sitting

against the wall. The Human stopped, and looked over to the Vulpian.

"You been down here long?" Amandrianna asked, which piqued Veralis's suspicion. She had been sprinting away with terror from Miles not moments ago, and now she looked as though nothing had happened.

"Not really," Veralis said. Having done a little research on the hurricane and flood that wrecked this town, she was able to quickly think up a cover story. "Just waiting for the planet techs to do their work."

"And how long have you been telling yourself that?" Amandrianna asked. It seemed as though she was expecting to hear an answer along the lines of years.

"Telling myself? This only happened about eight days ago, these things take time to do right." Veralis then stood up to face Amandrianna, but not with hostility, there was still an act to put on, after all.

"And how many months and years will that turn into where the 'Planet Techs' assure that it's in the works? How long will you have to—"

"This isn't the first time Mjarfus has had natural disasters! It might not be the last time this particular town gets bitten by them, but all the buildings are standing yet! It's not *ruined*, it's just evacuated for a bit! The rest of us are here now because we didn't want to live elsewhere for that time! Do you... do you not know

<GREGOR FJELLREV>

how this planet tends to work?" Veralis didn't say this with hostility or argument, but more like confusion, as if she was utterly perplexed by this creature that didn't understand the storm seasons on Mjarfus.

Amandrianna was the perplexed one in this situation, however, as Veralis knew exactly what she was doing. "How long does it take? How often are these disasters? Do you have equipment in your homes to be safe?" Amandrianna finally interrogated.

"From now, another six days at most to clear out the flood without ruining the entire forest not far from here. Maybe next time it'll only take six days overall," Veralis explained. "These disasters only actually get like this maybe once every six or seven years, and of course we have tools and supplies in our homes! Enough for ourselves and our neighbors! We've only lived here our whole lives, we're not stupid! Are you... surprised? Do I see surprise on your face?"

It seemed like somehow a sinister kind of surprise, like when someone finds out that they won't be able to manipulate another person as easily as they first thought.

"What... what are you?" Veralis asked, her eyes glowing a deep amber as her Psionic empathy pierced straight through Amandrianna Sarvalimil, and no secrets of who she was were hidden from Veralis.

"You..." Veralis growled, suddenly overcome with

rage. "You manipulative bitch! I'll kill you for all you've done!" Without even thinking, Veralis produced her twin axes and slashed at Amandrianna, who jumped back in surprise, and turned around to make her escape. Veralis was having none of it, and summoned a psionic barrier in front of Amandrianna's path. The Human turned around, a stern and huffy look on her face.

"You don't get to play by your rules," Veralis spat. "You fight on my field now."

She tossed the axe in her strong hand to Amandrianna, not even bothering to switch afterwards. The Human swung Veralis's own axe at her, only to be met with a quick parry, and a few more as Amandrianna Sarvalimil continued in vain to try to fight the Cynofrax Vulpian.

Veralis soon threw the other axe on the ground, and put her hands behind her back. Enraged, Amandrianna continued her attack, the assault was feral and untrained. It seemed Amandrianna was only even fighting because she wasn't getting her way like she thought she would. Veralis continued to evade the attacks before finally bringing her knee into Amandrianna's gut, then planting her foot into the solar plexus of her foe. Amandrianna gasped as she tried to recover her breath, and dropped her weapon before sprinting directly to the stone wall of the transit tunnel,

<GREGOR FJELLREV>

very deliberately pressing her back against it and putting her hands up.

"I surrender, I admit defeat," Amandrianna said in a quick and snappy tone. It seemed she expected Veralis to care about this deception.

"A hag like you would never truthfully surrender," Veralis said, pulling her axes back into her hands. "And I don't need to read your mind to know that you'd never admit to *shit*."

An axe heaved and embedded in her skull ended the life of Amandrianna Sarvalimil. Veralis threw the other at her lifeless body in disgust, yanking the pair from her corpse from the distance, and channeling a surge of power that burned off the blood, it didn't deserve to stain her steel. Veralis then turned around, only to see Miles Radien standing there... confused, it seemed. He looked at Amandrianna's corpse, then Veralis, and back and forth again. He was indeed confused.

"She was... evil! How could I *not?!*" Veralis exclaimed.

"That's not what confuses me, Veralis," Miles said. "You are correct. There's no doubt there."

"What, then?" Veralis still seemed to be recovering from what she saw when she looked into Amandrianna's mind. Miles just stood there, seemingly unable to even word what confused him so much. He looked over to the body of Amandrianna, and blinked slowly. He then closed his eyes with relief, and his shoulders relaxed as his sigh seemed to relieve him of a great weight carried for far too long.

"It's honestly for the better that I wasn't the one who killed her at last. What confuses me is the fact that this is what took place. The ideal solution... best-case scenario. Right all along."

"Sarvalimil, though... if her married surname was Radien, why did she take the alias Sarvalimil? If she was going around as Amandrianna Radien, she would've found you much more quickly!"

Miles shrugged. "I don't know. She was... a strange and particular kind of smart, idiotic and malicious all at the same time. Maybe her plan was to do something horrid as Amandrianna Sarvalimil, then reveal that she was my mother, and try to drag my name through the mud by association? I don't know."

"It's... a combination of thee names," Veralis pieced together. "Mil, as in Miles, but what are Val and Sar?"

Miles shrugged. "She had two sons and a daughter. I'm the youngest of the lot, and Sarena died when she was seventeen. But I hadn't heard from Valdres for years even before I encountered Melaqros on that first day."

Miles soon fell to his knees with joy and relief. "Veralis... thank you. Thank you so, so much."

"For ridding you of an old enemy?" Veralis said, resolutely.

"More than that." Miles began to walk back towards the Aura Runner, and Veralis quickly caught up.

"Radien, I looked into her mind and saw every reason you can't bring yourself to trust anyone, not even me..." Veralis said, putting a hand on Miles's shoulder, to his confusion.

"She wasn't the only one who taught me that, Veralis. I hope you don't think me so petty as to act the way I do all because of a single person." Miles explained, gently brushing off Veralis's hand, or handpaw, rather.

"I know," Veralis continued. "But in her I saw everyone else as well. I... you're a mystery to me, Radien. What even kept you going?"

"Spite," Miles admitted. "It's the greatest motivator in the universe. Spite will keep you alive when nothing else will, that sheer contempt for your enemies, and absolute will to not let them get to say they got you. I lived out of spite. I grew tired of it, but I kept doing it because I knew it worked. I counted the seconds until the minute, the hour and the day like I was in grade school again, and every moment I could acknowledge I was still awake and alive, that was one more moment I had earned despite everyone who would rather I stopped."

The two reached their ships, and Miles still stood there, a reflective look on his face. Unwavering, and staunchly not allowing himself to feel any different.

"Veralis, today you have done me an immeasurable favor, and I owe you a debt I can never repay. This is truly the first time I have felt joy in my life, to know that I was right all along on this. All the years I hated and despised everything she was, but I still knew that I couldn't be the one to kill her. Because then it would just be me. Just angry little Miles, being angry. But the wise man fears three things: The sunless day, the moonless night, and the anger of a kind person. I've known you to be as kind as you are wise, Veralis. And I couldn't think of a better person to rid me of Amandrianna Ra—"

Veralis shook her head as she cut off that sentence. "Such an evil person did not have the last name of Radien. That name is far too good for her. She died Sarvalimil, that will be the name of her dishonor. Not even the one she was born with."

As the Aura Runner made its way back to Cynofrax, Miles realized something else.

"Vulpians don't use the word evil lightly," he found himself remembering. "It's not an adjective casually used."

He then scoffed slightly, both satisfied and sorrowful in retrospect. "I really was right all along on this one, if nothing else. It's nice to know that... but I wish I didn't have to be so painfully correct."

ACT VI
FEAR NO MAN NOR BEAST,
ESPECIALLY NO GOD

You wanted to see me?" Miles asked, having answered the summons of the Aura Prism on Cynofrax.

"Yes..." the Prism's voice said, not with hesitation, but more as if it was still trying to process the event that led to needing Miles's presence. "There is a flaw in my memory, a flaw that needs rectification."

"I fail to see how I can help with that, but continue."

"Recorded history recounts the destruction of the Sehlsaln Anchor, but my personal memory errs in this regard. I see the events as though I live through them, and they do not take place as history remembers. If it were not for the fact that I also remember having once remembered these events correctly, I would call it benign. But I can see that my recollection of the Sehlsaln Anchor's destruction has been altered."

Miles still failed to see how he was to help with that.

"Miles Radien, you have no prior knowledge of the Sehlsaln Anchor, and I would send you into the memory of history, to play it out as it should be."

"I would think that my lack of knowledge on this is precisely why I should *not* try to fix it."

"If I were to tell you the opposite is the case, you would be quick to contradict me," the Prism correctly predicted. "But the reason I ask... it is hard to explain fully, but it is vital that you do not see it as a past to be preserved or corrected, but as a present to be acted within. You must act as you would, and that will ensure the repair of my memory for this event."

"I think I get it..." Miles started.

"Just... act natural, as it were," the Prism stated, and Miles nodded. As soon as he blinked, he found himself in an underground chamber with what looked like a small resistance group, and everything was bathed in an azure hue, likely from the crystal that was providing light.

"*Unsletts Arasehlakarka'e er Salnpas past Kunarel... The Lords of Evil have one connection remaining in the universe...*" one of the persons present said. Though his ears heard the Old Cynofraxian language, Miles still understood their meaning.

"The Aura does not translate, yet I still understand... These are the people precursor to the Vulpians..." Miles thought to himself, but did not speak.

"*Dwen Sehlsaln yasehlsentia ilakarzhernt uner iyezhernt. Siire seyt, Viun-Demons daant sa-eyva Sashals pasaked Unarel'e. This final anchor is particularly bitchy since it will destroy its destroyer. It seems to rely on this, and the Demons hope that we will value our lives over the universe's,*" the elder continued. Miles assumed he was either the leader or simply older than most of the others by his demeanor and lead of the meeting.

"*Su akar ald sehlka... Sa akaraln ohn zhernt. They're not wrong... we don't want to die,*" one of the Cynofraxians commented. "*Sa'e valtd yafakae, Sa'e ya-aldfakae, Sa sok tuuf nupas Gizul! Deyl ald ohn sehltayt elak sirth Gizul! We've fought long, we're so close, we can taste the new dawn! I don't want to lose the chance to see the dawn!*"

An air of dread fell over the room. Someone would have to be the last casualty of the War for Reality.

"*Deyl akaralr zhernt il! Deyl ohn siigiraont un Giraonen Sa Una fuuret! I won't die for this! I want to perform on the stage we all set!*" someone randomly called out to break the silence.

"*Shas sehldeyluna akar Duul?! How selfish are you?!*" Another called him out.

"*Akar Duul zhernt? Sii gifeina! Giyapasld! Iln Deyl akaraln seynt Er iye zhernr, una falil akara Deyl! Will you die, then? Feel free to! That is acceptable! If I don't need to be the one who dies, all the same to me!*" the one speaking his mind on self-preservation replied.

In a fit of frustration , Miles fired a bolt at this coward, this *Sehlkavihka* which smacked the back of his head against the wall, leaving him with at least a concussion, likely imminent death.

"*Deyl akar! I will!*" Miles shouted. All eyes turned to him. "*Deyl akar! Deyl kavih akarka tholn Ulk aldka dwenr! Sath ka deyl'e er Shal akara Una Shal? I will! I refuse to be why the war never ends! What is my one life to all life?*"

The room was still silent, and with that silence, Miles stormed out of the room, and out of the cave he and his comrades hid within, in the distance, seeing his quarry: The anchor. The final connection that the Demons had to reality, and its evil power seethed with its will to take whoever destroyed it with them.

"*Kanaveyn. So be it,*" he said as he drew his sword and started running towards the Demons guarding the anchor. It didn't take long for his charge to be noticed, but he didn't care. It's not like the Demons were ones for stealth these days. The tactics were simple but effective. With his approach, some of the Demon guards would break off to deal with him, and he'd cut them down as they were separate from their comrades. As much as they could move forward faster than he could step back, he didn't need to outpace them, just outfight them. Gradually chiseling away at the contingent, they could not replace their numbers faster than Miles could dispatch them. This last anchor could only safely bring in a few demons an hour, let they risked destroying it themselves. And Miles was definitely killing more than a few per hour.

Surprisingly, this tactic continued to work even as the Demons surely must have known was his plan was. But Miles wasn't one to complain about when a plan was working. The last of the Anchor's guards fell, and he approached the sinister structure.

The actual gate that the Demons traveled through wasn't much more than a crackling crimson portal, but it was what kept it open that meant it was so unstable and demanding of energy. With the Aura Prism having just been forged, the barriers it was keeping had to be broken through, and this was no small task, let alone keeping such a breach open.

"Threytn Deyl'e dwen zhernt Sehlkulk... novos yagitay. If it means I am the last to die in this cursed war...

no greater honor." The sword in his hand became a battleaxe as Miles began to understand who he was reliving the final moments of, and swung it at one of the anchor pinions. A great shooting pain rocketed up both arms as if his very bones rebelled against what he was doing. But this served only to anger him into further action, and he swung again, shattering the tethering crystal. The Taigron Kirinaultr dropped her battleaxe. Her arms were broken, but there was still one more tethering crystal to destroy. She walked over, staring it down, refusing to grant it one inch of satisfaction from the pain she endured in the name of destroying this last gate to Hell.

"*Duul akar sehltaytd! You are defeated!*" were the final words of Kirinaultr as she swung her leg against the crystal, shattering it with a decisive and raging kick, and everything turned to white as the explosion ended the pain.

Miles found himself back on The Mountain, panting heavily. He tensed up his left arm, just to make sure it still worked. It did. "What... what about that memory was wrong?!"

"The Defender who sacrificed herself, when I beheld the flawed memory, I could not remember if it was her I saw. But it is known, plain as the day, that Kirinaultr's last act was to end the First War for Reality.

But now I do see that as clearly as I should."

Miles still was catching his breath. "I don't think this is something that should be so easily moved on from. If you couldn't remember what you should of Kirinaultr's sacrifice, there may be something else at work here. Unless of course, a prism forged of cosmic power can get Alzheimer's after however many billion years."

"Indeed, my memory should not be alterable."

"Well, then maybe you should look into why it was for a moment."

Miles began to walk away, still stretching his arms and legs from the aftermath of reliving Kirinaultr's final moments.

"Radien," the Prism said, and he turned around again. "I must say, I am glad you're not a god-fearing type. I can think of many who, if I asked this of them, would do so with flowery praise and a refusal to advise me."

"Any god to be feared is no god at all. It is Demons who demand fear," Miles remarked as he headed off and back to his home.

By the time he got home, he was able to thoroughly convince himself that his arms and legs were fine now. He then pulled up a few planetary maps, one of Homphalion, another of Raon-Arashal, and one more of Korvideyl Moon. He was searching for a suitable build location for the base that Micah had talked to him about. He had considered Turazin, but later figured that if SWEEPS ever abandoned its base, he'd just commandeer that rather than build an entire new one. Strangely enough, there was a rather promising-looking location on Raon-Arashal deep within one of its most inhospitable areas, the Kaladorum Black Zone. The reason it was promising was due to being a sort of border area between natural biomes, the conflicting temperature and weather pattern made the terrain and local flora much tamer by comparison, so it would be possible to secure an area to build such a base within. More likely a fortress than regular old base, since it would practically need to be clawed from the hands of the Devouring Jungle itself. But it would be possible to not only do this, but with some of the construction technology the Death World Vulpians used in their permanent cities, it would be feasible to build such a fortress and maintain it.

Miles opened a channel with Micah. "Micah? I think I might have a location for that base of yours."

When she arrived to discuss further, Miles had already worked further on the concept, drafting out the effective area the base could be built within, and started drawing some basic blueprints.

"The main challenge is simply making the area safe to build within, but the fact of the varying climate conditions in that area means that during the orbital year, there's a window of about sixteen days where this is achievable due to the sort of 'transition' period between the deadly flora and fauna of one season and the deadly flora and fauna of the next. It would be during this time that I would lend the use of my Keystone Forge to start laying foundations and securing the area so that construction would be able to continue beyond this brief point of opportunity," Miles explained.

Micah certainly hoped it was as promising as it looked. "My only concern is the scale you're planning to build on. We'd be looking at building what amounted to basically an entire castle in the middle of the Kaladorum Black Zone."

"I thought about that," Miles said excitedly. "I've been programming the base layout itself into my Keystone forge, so that once the area itself is physically stable, I can then immediately use its Matter Projector to spit out this foundation that will keep the area safe to build on. Once I finish the programming, it's just a matter of having enough... whatever to construct enough of the material I'm using."

"And what are you using?"

Miles brought up a molecular composition map for the kind of brick the fortress would be made from. "Kendradeyne's scientists have been experimenting with

<FIRE TO BURN THE STARS>

a material they've called 'Dredgestone.' Not only is it dense enough as a molecular structure to be almost completely weatherproof to Raon-Arashal's conditions, it's also relatively light as a brick-like material. That way, you're not restricted to building solely on bedrock lest you risk total geological collapse." The brick form of the Dredgestone was jet-black, which seemed to be a plus on aesthetics. "With a Dredgestone base and a coating of the weatherproofing compound that keeps Kendradeyne stable, this base is nigh impenetrable for even the Kaladorum Black Zone"

"And what's the catch?" Micah asked.

"The amount of raw material I'd need to do the projection is more than the Keystone Forge can keep in reserves. At full capacity, it'd be able to make about a third of this from a single sustained construction period. Which means... that during the construction, I'd need a consistent influx of more raw material. But I have a solution for that as well, one that even acts as a positive diplomatic measure."

Miles then turned on a screen that showed several massive landfills on Earth, and the locations of underground nuclear waste disposal sites.

"I built the Fourteen Werewolves on Earth out of raw trash, and I only had an Atomic Forge at the time, not a full-on Keystone Forge. I built a brick and mortar

<GREGOR FJELLREV>

building out of refuse, and I'll bet it made someone who worked at that landfill happy that several tons of garbage just vanished without trace or consequence. There's a fucking island of trash the size of England in the ocean, and to one's surprise, it's not England itself." Miles then chuckled a bit as his admittedly low-hanging fruit of a joke. "Just set up a warp channel between the build site and a big fuck-off collection of waste, and we knock down two massive birds with one stone. And to top it off, the Humans will definitely appreciate the fixer-upper."

Micah seemed surprised that the Earth had that much raw waste, even for a planet that didn't have recycling technology on the level of Atomic Reassignment. By her logic, they should've been at least able to do something useful. Miles was not surprised at her own, making a few easily-made comments comparing human nature to the trash heaps themselves.

Regardless, they made the plans to construct the base as soon as that sixteen-day window opened up, and by the time they went their separate ways for until then, had already marked which landfills and nuclear waste disposal bunkers to empty for the raw atomic material.

Miles had been experimenting with a new function for his scanner/comm-link device, programming a unique alerting system for if a Demonic or Void incursion was taking place and a general call for assistance in dealing with it was being sent. The clue that he had successfully integrated this function was the unique tone he had configured for such general calls, and the fact that it had just gone off.

VOID INCURSION

KILLENTARN, GLASS REFLEX SYSTEM

CALL MADE BY: FLEETGAME (ASCENDANT CITY)

"Oh, good. That works," Miles said. "Techbooth, start up the Aura Runner and find out where on Killentarn that Void Incursion is happening."

By the time Miles got to the Aura Runner, he had the location of the Void Incursion, a wilderness area on Killentarn about a hundred kilometers from the small town of Fleetgame. After landing just outside the town, Miles made his way towards the defensive position set up by local militia.

"What can you tell me?" Miles asked an Ascendant named Dawnfang, who seemed to be in charge of the surprisingly well-armed militia.

"The Voidspawns have been more or less poking about, trying to see where they can set up their holdpoint. This is the closest settlement to the gate itself, so they will inevitably make their move here," Dawnfang explained.

"Is there a reason the Voidspawns don't try to set

<GREGOR FJELLREV>

themselves up in that wildlife sanctuary itself? Or just right where they land in general?"

Dawnfang scoffed. "The Voidspawns are a stubbornly procedural lot, if that makes sense. They seem to prefer to seize settled areas beyond anything else. They never register wildlife as the threat to them."

"I wonder if these guys have heard of Christopher Anvil..." Miles muttered, to which Dawnfang looked exceptionally confused. "Uh... Human author. The Gentle Earth, specifically. Good read."

The Ascendant sheriff nodded, and Miles conjured his Orvitarian Collapse Rifle and set it to long-range mode. Through the scope, he saw the Voidspawn scouts that Dawnfang had mentioned.

"There doesn't seem to be too many of them..." Miles noted, before turning to Dawnfang. "Do you guys have a Counter-Catalyst for the Void Rift?"

Dawnfang nodded, handing Miles a glowing green crystal. "We were planning on waiting for our special ops boys to get this done, but if you can close that gate, I'll gladly let you do just that right now. Get that crystal within fifty meters of the gate, and it'll start working. The closer the better."

Miles nodded. "I won't let you down, Sheriff."

"My name is Dawnfang."

"In that case, I won't let you down, Dawnfang."

Miles then fired three shots, each into three different patrolling Voidspawns, and running off into the forest.

"Was anyone else expecting him to grab a few of you guys to head with him?" Dawnfang asked to a few of the Militia, who subsequently nodded, seemingly confused at the absence of this request.

Miles, however, was already well into the thicket. Stopping near the clearing that the Void Rift made, Miles allowed his second sight to show him where the Voidspawns were. Just before raising his rifle to fire on his first target, he felt a sharp pain in his right shoulder. One of the buggers had snuck up behind him and drove a spike down his arm. Cursing, Miles blasted the Voidspawn with a wave of power from his left hand, and when the creature disintegrated in its death throes, the spike in his shoulder vanished, leaving the wound open.

"That... actually would've really worked. Thank the gods I'm left-handed, though..." Miles winced as the heightened regeneration capabilities of The Aura mended him. Though not a stranger to using his power in this manner, it never was a comfortable process, though by the same token, it wasn't searingly painful.

Miles lined up his shot again, but suddenly was yanked backwards and slammed into a tree. Another Voidspawn had appeared near him.

"Okay, how are you buggers appearing *right*

behind me if the rift is over *there?*" Miles spat, groaning as his floating rib stitched back together. The Voidspawn fired bolts of its eldritch-resemblant energy at Miles, and he conjured a shield. However, this shield was almost completely overtaken by the Voidspawn's assault, with no small discomfort for the shield-bearer himself. Miles drew his pistol with his free hand and quickly fired three shots into the Voidspawn, destroying it.

"Okay, right. My power comes from the ever-present flow of energy in the universe, and these guys aren't exactly from the area. Got it. Learning as I go."

Another Voidspawn approached, but Miles was ready this time with his cutlass, deflecting the shots fired and running it through. He then felt an impact at his back. He was starting to draw the attention of everyone here.

"All right, to hell that nice, clean plan I had!" Miles declared, charging forward with a yell, and cutting down the Voidspawns that tried to stop him. Miles continued to fight his way forward, several minutes later able to see the tear in reality that was letting outsiders in. He grabbed the Counter-Catalyst from his pocket, and heaved it at the Rift, and as the crystal traveled through the air, it began to glow brighter as it approached the gate, soon exploding in a blinding flash of light. When Miles uncovered his eyes, he saw there were no more

Voidspawns, and the Rift had been sealed.

When he got back to Fleetgame, Miles met up with Dawnfang to report the success of his mission, and the regrettable loss of the Counter-Catalyst.

"You got the Rift closed, though. We'll gladly take that," Dawnfang said with relief. "It'll take a bit to get a new Counter-Catalyst, but we'll do it."

"Happy to help, Dawnfang," Miles replied. "Anything else I can assist with?"

Dawnfang thought for a moment as Miles worked on the drink one of the locals had bought for him. "There's no rush on this, but one of my friends in Niflus City said that he was investigating something. Something apparently potentially big, and I haven't heard from him since, and that was two months ago."

Miles downed the rest of his drink, and stood up, but Dawnfang slowed him down. "He's still around, Radien. That particular investigation just took a back seat, so no need to worry. Besides, that's only the second drink that's been paid for."

"Well, that sounds like a challenge to me," Miles said, looking at the empty bottom of his glass.

"Though I can't help but wonder, Radien..." Dawnfang started. "You charged off into the forest on your own to face the Voidspawns. You didn't point at a couple of us, who would've gone with you and said 'you guys, with me.' You didn't even look like you planned to."

"Well, that is because I didn't plan to." Miles simply replied. "I was willing to handle it myself, and not put your men in danger."

"Radien, I and every militiaman here in Fleetgame understand those risks. You could've asked *me* to come with you, and I would've done it. I wouldn't have minded dying in a fight that meant the Rift was closed."

"Are you criticizing me, Dawnfang?" Miles asked sternly. "Are you saying I should have asked men I don't even know the names of to quite possibly die with me?"

Dawnfang shook his head, apologizing. "I'm not sure what I'm thinking on the matter, sorry. I suppose we all were expecting you to, and are not sure what to do since you didn't."

Miles forgave Dawnfang quickly enough. "Today is a victory, Dawnfang. Everybody lived! Let there be rejoicing!"

And thus, there was much rejoicing upon the reminder of this fact. At least, for a a little under an hour. But something was definitely wrong, and Miles could feel the tension in the air.

"Dawnfang, why are all the Varok-Torividan here so damn tense?" Miles finally asked.

"Well, we just got over a Void Incursion, things still need to wind down a little."

<FIRE TO BURN THE STARS>

Miles shook his head. "The Incursion is *over*, Dawnfang. These men and women are clearly not concerned about that anymore. This is the kind of tension that has existed for a solid while."

Dawnfang sat there in his seat across from Miles, then sighed. "Leave it, Radien."

Miles stood up quickly. "I will do no such thing, especially considering that you have just told me to."

Dawnfang then stood up to meet him, drawing a pistol from his hip. Miles yanked it from Dawnfang's hand, firing three times. Two in the chest, one in the head, dropping the Ascendant just as quickly as he had once raised a glass with him. Three other Ascendant and two Varok-Torividan drew their weapons at this, and Miles responded by shooting down one of the reptilians and wounding an Ascendant. Everyone else quickly scrambled out of the bar, which gave Miles the clearance he needed to send a rippling wave of Aura energy across the room, shattering the cover of his foes, and tearing the wounded Ascendant to scrap.

With another surge of Miles's power, all the guns in the room jammed, and the fight moved to melee as he tore the arm off the last Ascendant and caved in the head of the inbound Varok-Torividan with it, then kicking his lifeless opponents out of the way. The last one soon had his own knife embedded in his weapon arm, and Miles pinned him to the wall.

"You have very little time to explain yourself," Miles growled.

"You have very little time left alive, standing against Regime like this."

Miles coldly dug his thumb into the wound on the Varok-Torividan's arm, and illicited a pained yell.

"Answer my question truthfully and I may let you live. Is the Regime the reigning totalitarian fascist government here on Killentarn?"

"Reigning, yes. But you choose the words of—"

Miles swiftly jammed the knife into the Regime pig's head, not intending to let him finish that sentence. Miles exited the bar, met by the armed militia that had previously been defending the town from the Voidspawns. Or more likely, just themselves, with no real care of anyone else.

"You guys had better tell me that you didn't know they were Regime, or—"

A few moments later, Miles entered the communications office in Fleetgame, grumbling heavily while covered in the blood of Varok-Torividan and Ascendant Vital Fluid. "Fucking regimes, man," he grumbled as with Techbooth's assistance, he disengaged the dampers that prevented a planetwide broadcast.

"My name is Miles Sorvenjar Radien, and I am

making an open address to all Regime-aligned individuals, whether directly you are a part of it, or indirectly support its continued existence. I'm coming for you. If I have to tear you all to shreds myself, I'll do that, but hopefully my actions will spawn a resistance soon enough to aid me here. I lived on a planet that loved killing its people with a slow grind into oblivion that got good men to kill themselves long enough to have no patience for the fascist or the authoritarian. And with my power, I now can rain hell upon every last one of you. I recently learned not long ago that after first contact with the Conclave on my home world, there was a short but potent worldwide revolution that specifically targeted the ruling classes. Politicians and oligarchs alike were lynched and guillotined by my people who understood that the scum of the Earth could not be allowed any chance to leave it. I'm going to fight the civil war on Killentarn I never got to on Earth, and you will all learn very harshly the brutality I reserve for the foes of mine that think themselves invincible."

Miles terminated the transmission, and left the station. As he had requested of them, everyone living in the town of Fleetgame was waiting outside.

"The Regime's presence in Fleetgame is currently eliminated. But that's going to change in a matter of hours. They'll be crawling all over here looking for me, and without a doubt plan to kill every single one of you just for existing near me. My ship has room for all of you, and will pilot itself to Turazin, where I have people waiting to find you new homes, and new lives. If you want escape, the time to do that is right now. If you want to stay here, you *must* be ready to fight," Miles said to everyone.

One of the Varok-Torividan spoke up. "Can your ship get out of orbit without getting gunned down? The Regime has been blowing up attempted escapees with those 'defense satellites'"

"I've not seen a satellite around any planet I've been to that can get through the Aura Runner's cloak," Miles assured. "Even then, the shields will repel any assault the Regime tries to throw at it."

Murmurs in the crowd seemed to believe Miles was telling the truth. The Aura Runner then decloaked in the town square, to their surprise, and Miles's point. About seventy percent of the civilians then immediately boarded the ship via the cargo door Miles had added that led to the bigger-on-the-inside section of the Aura Runner, a few stragglers making the decision to later. Miles looked to the hundred or so that seemed to be planning to stay behind.

"You realize the choice you're making," Miles commented.

"That's why we're making it. I suppose all it's taken is someone to show us they can be bested in combat."

"They were shit fighters, why else do you think they carried five weapons each?" Miles smirked, and ordered the Aura Runner to warp to Turazin, and deliver a message to the Conclave regarding Killentarn's Regime.

Wasting no time afterwards, Miles and the townsfolk began to arm themselves for the battle ahead, first raiding the Regime Guard station for its weapons and munitions.

"Remember, you don't need seven guns, you need one gun you can use well and a lot of ammo," Miles reminded as he and the others inventoried their munitions.

After setting up their internal comms, Miles worked to prepare a Defense Grid around Fleetgame to prevent them from being shelled from the air. A few minutes after that, an explosion was absorbed by the shield, which held steady.

"And that's why you use a Defense Grid when you're planning to get sieged," Miles commented. "Open windows in the grid at ground level at each of the three entrances into the area! We gotta give them an opening so that they don't make their own! And make them generous, because I am indeed issuing a challenge!"

Miles's comm-link pinged, and it was Xenidar.

"Don't you dare tell me I can't be doing this, Xenidar," Miles sternly said as he calibrated the Orvitarian Collapse Rifle.

"I sure hope you don't think of me as that close to Human, Radien," Xenidar said. "The Conclave has suspected Killentarn's Regime for some time now, there just hadn't been a way to solidly prove that they were as... existent as they are. With the refugees and your message on the Aura Runner, Arch-Militant Wöllschlager already has a blockade around the planet, to make sure no leaders escape. The only reason he's not putting boots on the ground right now is because he doesn't want to risk mistaken identities and friendly fire."

"Acknowledged, Xenidar." Miles looked through the scope of his rifle and saw a long-range scanner had been set up on the outskirts of town, well beyond the shield. He then turned to the Ascendant that was passing him. "You, what's your name?"

"Render," he replied.

"All right, Render. I want you on broadcast duty. You gotta be letting the whole planet know that we're alive, and that we're still fighting, no matter what the Regime's propaganda machines spit out. They might be saying we've already been killed and the town is retaken."

<FIRE TO BURN THE STARS>

"I can do that!" Render then ran towards the planetary comms station in town.

"I want at least twelve guarding the comm station!" Miles ordered, and volunteers quickly moved. "Xenidar, can you patch me to Arch-Militant Wöllschlager?"

"Already on it." A few moments later, Jarrek was onscreen in the Redarian Interplanetary Battlefleet's flagship, *Spear of The Velani*.

"Arch-Militant, I know you've got those ships making sure the Regime doesn't escape, but you're gonna have refugees trying to make a run for it in the opportunity of the chaos." Miles informed.

Jarrek nodded. "We've already taken down the weapon satellites. Any non-combat ships that come up are getting snared and turned upside-down for infiltrators. We'll handle things up here, you focus on the ground."

"Watch your flank too, Jarrek. The civil unrest on Killentarn is why the Voidspawns thought they could open a rift here. I wouldn't put it beyond them to try again, or the Demons to see if they can show everyone how it's done."

Jarrek acknowledged, and terminated the comm-link. Miles then got the attention of everyone with him.

"Ladies, gentlemen, and all other configurations

of being, whether or not this works for all of Killentarn is squarely on us. Remember this above all else: The only thing that can stop you from fighting is death, and every breath you take is a breath you've earned in spite of your enemy. For every second that you can observe that you are still awake and alive, you're winning. Every moment, every instant is another that proves that you have yet to be beaten. As long as you can breathe, you can fight. As long as you can breathe, you have not been defeated. And as long as you can remember that, this fight is still being fought!"

The Ascendant, Varok-Torividan and scattered Loriken listened intently.

"The Regime is not an enigma. They are not infinite. There is a number that represents the amount of people that are a part of the Regime, and that number can only go down! Every kill is a permanent blow to them! Every wounded is however many weeks it takes for recovery! All we have to do is not stop fighting!"

A hearty cheer from the crowd, and Miles still had one last thing to say as another explosive shell was absorbed by the Defense Grid.

"Killentarn stands!"

"Killentarn stands!" the defenders yelled back.

"Killentarn stands!" Miles cheered again.

"Killentarn stands!"

Miles hopped down from his vantage with a final send-off. "So til Valhalla, or let us drag them to Helheim!" To a resounding battlecry from everyone around him.

Soon, everyone had taken their positions. The bombs stopped being thrown against the Defense Grid, and the Regime stormtroopers were moving in. "Aura guide me, through friend and foe alike, that I may emerge in great victory." Miles muttered to himself before firing the first shot at the approaching Regime pigs.

When they realized they were under attack, they quickly began to throw down their portable barricades and dig in. Several dozen at least were eliminated in this first firefight as Miles then ordered everyone to save their ammo unless they had a clear shot. It seemed the Regime wanted to either wait them out, or find another way in. Miles quickly ran to the Defense Grid generator, and extended the shield to underground to prevent tunneling. About an hour later, he and Fleetgame's defenders felt a tremor originating from just outside the Defense Grid.

"I knew that was a good idea," Miles commented to himself.

"How did you know they were going to tunnel?" a Varok-Torividan by the name of Tsaruc asked Miles.

"It's an authoritarian regime. They'll do anything

<GREGOR FJELLREV>

to not have to work towards a win they feel entitled to."

Scattered skirmishes of maybe a few shots each continued throughout the day, but without any real progress by either side. A few of the defenders had managed to knock off a Regime trooper here and there, and progress was progress.

"Every step forward is very much that," Miles reiterated to his battle brothers after night fell on their half of Killentarn. "It takes years of training and a lifetime of conditioning before the Regime puts a weapon in any of their operative's hands. Each one dead is that many years and that much money down the tubes for them. It'll add up."

During that night, Miles and a few others who weren't actively keeping watch had some well-earned food and drink at the storehouse where all the rations throughout town had been consolidated, and Miles sat alone, reading some information that Techbooth had sent his comm-link. One of the Varok-Torividan sat across from him.

"I'm sure you've heard it a lot already, but I thank you for showing us that we *can* fight them."

"It's no problem, especially as it's true," Miles replied with a nod. "I've been reading up a little on the Kalvak Nakaen, apparently the elite policing arm of the Killentarn Regime."

"Damn, sure hope we don't have to face them."

"According to information, no force of any size has lasted any longer than an hour in a standoff with the Kalvak Nakaen. I'm reading up on 'em because those were the guys we were facing today."

Several heads that overheard the conversation turned, as did Miles's new drinking partner.

"The Regime first tried to claim that the Kalvak Nakaen retook Fleetgame inside ten minutes. Our boys in orbit responded by broadcasting a live feed of us still in the town. Then the Regime tried to say that they didn't actually send the *actual* Kalvak Nakaen, it was just an independent cell of pro-Regime militants with similar gear. I'll bet you can imagine how well that's turning out for them, especially since y'know, people are dead and those people have names that are associated with a position usually regarded with great pride."

Miles chuckled. "No one apparently could last an hour against 'em. We're about to enter day two, no casualties on our side. And I'd say we've iced at least thirty of theirs."

This seemed to invigorate everyone as the word traveled among the defenders of Fleetgame. They had taken down at least thirty of what was supposed to be the best of the Regime's best. That meant that they were better shots and better fighters than at least thirty of the

Kalvak Nakaen. The confidence they gained didn't make them cocky by any means, but their actions would undoubtedly be much more decisive now.

Morning eventually came without incident. Perhaps the Kalvak Nakaen were too used to the privilege of sleeping through the night to have considered attacking during it. Miles scanned the temporary encampment, and found the life signs within were pulling back. Not believing the Kalvak Nakaen were really planning to retreat, Miles quickly gained contact with Jarrek in orbit.

"Jarrek, do you have an explanation for why the Kalvak Nakaen just pulled out of here?" Miles asked cautiously.

"The Regime's forces have consolidated at the Palace of Slaynvarra, and with the support of the Redarian Militarium, their final stand won't last long."

Miles looked towards an Ascendant, hoping for some context.

"The palace of Slaynvarra is essentially the Regime's big temple of... jerking each other off to themselves," the Ascendant responded. "If they were to make a final stand, they'd rather be slowly hunted down for sport than not make it there."

Miles nodded, and let Fleetgame's defenders know that he was headed to help finish off the Regime, and anyone else was welcome to come with him before he briefed Jarrek on his plan to do so.

"Good hunting, Radien," Jarrek responded, to Miles's confusion.

"What, you're not gonna tell me something stupid like 'this isn't your fight, Radien?'" was his retort.

"Why the hell would I do that? You made it your fight, and to top it off, you've fought it well."

Miles chuckled. "Thank you, Jarrek. Really." Then ended the transmission. "No sense in wasting time, boys, let's move!"

The city of Slaynvarra itself wasn't in total anarchy, but firefights were all over the place, as Miles told the fighters that came with him that they could go where they figured they were needed. The only buildings that had been burned were government ones, and corporate towers. Groups and individuals weren't patrolling the streets as much as searching for Regime pigs to clean up before the final assault on the palace began. Nobody wanted to get flanked during that. Miles soon met up with Svaynva, the Varok-Torividan in charge of the resistance siege camp in front of the palace, along the way luring a few pairs of loyalists into the buildings and alleys to fight them hand-to-hand, and easily kill them since they couldn't just shoot in such close quarters.

<GREGOR FJELLREV>

"We've secured the subterranean escape tunnels, and I've been in close contact with Arch-Militant Wöllschlager about monitoring their potential orbital escape. They know they're trapped in that ivory tower, and my best guess is that they're hoping to die of old age before we find our chance to get in. The only reason we don't just blast the tower to rubble is because the damn thing is tall, and there's no telling what collateral damage might happen. Not to mention that's where all the Regime's supply hordes are. They'd be helpful in rebuilding," Svaynva explained.

Miles peered over the cover and immediately was met with a bullet to his shoulder. Ducking back down, his power healed him quickly enough with a bit of concentration. "Auto-turrets?"

"Honestly? I wish. But no, that's the Golden Guard, and they're as obnoxiously well-armed as the name suggests."

Miles thought for a moment. "Have we got artillery, ordinance, or even just some grenades to chuck at 'em?"

"The problem is the one-way Defense Grid they have over the entire palace. They can shoot out from it, but not much is getting in," Svaynva replied.

"Aren't one-way Defense Grids an illegal weapons tech?"

"Fascist regimes are also illegal, but that sure didn't stop them because it's not like it wasn't working."

"Hard to believe this place once ratified the Pillars Three," Miles remarked.

"And no wonder they got their foothold because of it. No one suspected it could happen here, and that's exactly why it did."

"You'll have no argument from me, Svaynva. But right now, we gotta figure out how to get past that Defense Grid."

Miles ran through ideas that came to him as they did, such as finding the Defense Grid's resonant frequency. Of course, modern Defense Grids have constantly modulating frequencies as a result of the relative ease at which a person can acquire a resonator. The idea to call upon an ancient ritual dueling law that not even the leaders dared defy also fell flat because of the fact that they absolutely would defy it.

"Just how much punishment *can* that Defense Grid take?" Miles asked.

"A good barrage from orbit, but it'd be a close shave."

Miles immediately contacted Jarrek.

"Jarrek, I need a high-precision surgical strike on the coordinates I'm giving you." Miles said as he marked the landing pad on top of the building. Not the entire roof, Miles was going to make them divert enough power to the top of the grid to weaken the bottom enough for a breach.

"All right... *Spear of the Velani's* Prismatic Beam can make that happen for you. Setting target now."

"Fire when ready, Arch-Militant."

From high orbit, a powerful laser fired upon the top of the palace's Defense Grid, and started attempting to burn though. Miles read on his scanner that the shield's power was being slowly diverted to compensate, but inevitably, there would be a drop of the barrier at ground level to switch to one of the auxiliary power draws. Miles knew where the three Golden Guardsmen were positioned, and was ready when the barrier had to fall entirely at the lower third of the building. He quickly whipped out from cover and blasted each of the Golden Guards with bolts of The Aura's power, punching holes straight through their armors, and their chests. Miles then sprinted towards the palace itself, using The Aura to shield himself from a hail of bullets and plasma shots. The Defense Grid's faltering soon corrected itself, but not before Miles had dove though into the palace's threshold. Conjuring a spike in one hand and keeping his barrier up with the other, Miles threw the conjured Aura dart into the head of one Golden Guard, before finally releasing all the bullets his barrier had soaked up directly at the other, shredding both armor and flesh.

"I'm in!" Miles said on comm-link to Svaynva and Jarrek.

"Well, he's in," Svayvna acknowledged. "Arch-Militant, disengage that Prismatic Beam!"

Jarrek shut off the weapon's power as the forces on the ground planned a potential new way in to assist Miles, who was already carving a path of blood and Ascendant Vital Fluid towards the Hall of Opulence, where the leaders of the Regime hoped to live out the rest of their days before Killentarn's people could have their way. With a trail of dead Golden Guards behind him, Miles stood next to the door he had lined with Psionic charges, ready to blow the disgustingly fancy metalwork to smithereens. He then giggled to himself as he held his rifle.

"I've always wanted to do this!"

The door exploded, and Miles burst into the throne room with dozens of oligarchs and fascist thieves of the people, his rifle lighting up the scene. Having switched it to fully automatic, he mowed down the dictators and the authoritarians without mercy. A few tried to crawl away, whom he quickly executed. Less than two minutes later, there was a single Varok-Torividan cowering behind the gem-forged throne. Miles ordered him to come out of hiding.

"I do hope you're considered the head of state for Killentarn by this formerly living lot," Miles remarked, hoping he had saved the best for last.

"I am!" the Varok-Torividan snapped with both fear and toddler-like anger that he was no longer in power. "I am Ultimus Mirmakahrnaen!" Mirmakahrnaen then adjusted his robes as if his gestures were typically met with throngs taking a knee. "And if you don't—"

Miles cut off Mirmakahrnaen's sentence with a shot to his shoulder, and the former ruler screeched in pain. "The gods know what you've done here today, you uncouth rebel!"

"Any of the ones I'd give the time of day to are smiling upon me! Can you say the same of any god?!" Miles spat, pulling from his belt a knife instead of his cutlass, and driving it down into Mirmakahrnaen's unwounded shoulder, dragging it across his back before kicking the wretch to the ground. He then threw the knife, and another conjured one into each of Mirmakahrnaen's legs, and pulled them down and through the once-untouchable's feet with The Aura before finally silencing the cries of the man-child with a final spike through the throat, the screams turning into curdled coughs and last breaths. Miles stood over Mirmakahrnaen, staring into his terrified eyes as they slowly drained of life.

"Gods do not demand fear. Demons do, defeated coward. That will be your name as you wander the grey plains of purgatory until the end of Time, as a thousand choruses mock you endlessly, and call you by your name: Defeated. Coward. Defeated, coward..."

Finally, Mirmakahrnaen died. After lowering the Defense Grid around the Palace of Slaynvarra, the warriors of Killentarn quickly moved in and cleaned up any of the Golden Guards Miles had missed.

"Some might think you stole a pound of flesh from Killentarn's people," Svaynva commented, regarding how Miles was the one to end the life of the tyrant. "But if it weren't for you, he'd've died an old man with his boots still on the necks of the people he owed it to. You got us to start fighting proper at last, you might as well be the one who opens the door for us to get things right this time."

"Mirmakahrnaen wanted it all, even in death," Miles stated. "He wanted to be taken prisoner and paraded through the streets in a golden cage as jubilant throngs celebrated the capture of the... whatever his bullshit title was. He wanted his crimes read to him, etched on a marble tablet lined with jewels, inscribed with an iridium chisel. He wanted ten speeches all about how detestable he was before the gilded executioner's axe cleanly carved off his head into an ebony bucket, and with his head and the bucket enshrined in separate diamond-glass display cases in a museum of the dictator. And so I denied him that. I denied him the glorious death and immortality he thought he deserved, and gave him the one he really did." Miles's words were laced with disdain, and the relief that he prevented them from becoming reality.

"True as all that is, I still understand why some will undoubtedly be upset." He continued. "I wonder how many people who wanted nothing more than to fight never actually ended up doing that, by way of... circumstance. Fighters, warriors, who may very well have left their homes and gone to the cities, hoping to find a few Regime pigs to finally use their martial prowess on, but for some reason there just happened to be no patrols and no activity wherever they were that day. How many fighters didn't just not get to fight... How many somehow managed to never have the chance? How many were involuntarily pacifist?"

Svayvna seemed confused as to why those were the people Miles was thinking about.

"A planet connected, where you can hear the screams from a continent away... where the fire was everywhere *except* where you could actually help put it out. Not even smoke. Not even the smell of gunpowder or the sound of shots in the distance. Both there to see it

<FIRE TO BURN THE STARS>

all, and so far away that you can't do a damn thing. How many times did the warriors only get to watch, what they knew they could have done so much better? How many of them went mad? How many died by their own hands, so thoroughly denied not just peaceful existence, but the chance to fight for it? How many stories were stolen by way of never being permitted the opportunity to be made? How many ballads lost their heroes because the heroes never got their chance?"

Miles's voice was heavy, and his breath was pained.

"Do me a favor and find those people, Svayvna. Find them, and make sure they have a chance to know victory before the end."

Miles eventually headed to his home on Cynofrax for some Soup for the Darkness.

"I'm not even sure if I have any right to no longer be among them," he finished.

ACT VII
BETRAYAL ON KALIVAN TOR

The scanner and comm-link in Miles's pocket pinged. Specifically, it pinged the ping that pings when Jaden was the one pinging it.

"What do you need?" Miles asked, opening the channel.

"My lab assistant to not be a complete dunce would be a start." The yellow-furred Laksorian answered. "But what I'm calling you about is something I need for the GAMA device."

"I thought you finished that and even ran successful tests?" Miles questioned.

"Well, nothing wrong with heightening efficiency, is there?" Jaden clarified. "Honestly, I don't need it as much as 'understand that it would be really useful to have.'"

With that, Miles received a file on the comm-link detailing what Jaden was after, something called the

Elurian Karma Scale.

"The Elurians, as you might know, were a type of feline species that went extinct at the hands of Caltoran after... well, Caltoran. Though Eluria and Kendrosium weren't the only civilizations destroyed by him, they were the most prominent ones, and the boldest move by the Dark Six that unfortunately worked. The Scale is an artifact that particularly contributed to the fall of Eluria and its people, because, well, it's one of those 'comes with a price' artifacts, with enough obnoxious caveats that would make a Djinn uncomfortable. Regardless, there's definitely Elurian blood on it, and likely the only surviving samples left in creation."

"So... you don't even need the scale?"

"Gods, no! That thing in no small part led to the death of a whole species! You think I wanna try my luck with that? No, the Elurians were well-known as potent Psionics, and their blood was actually laced with raw cosmic power. Something allowed Elurian DNA and Psionic power to intertwine, and that bridge is in their blood, that unfortunately, all of it was spilled before I could figure this out and do anything about it. But if that Karma Scale is still in one piece, there's definitely surviving samples on it."

"Where would that even lead?"

"If I found out what actually allowed the Elurians

to have power literally running through their veins, I could extrapolate it into the GAMA's genetic re-coding process to integrate it into existing species, which would allow their power-wielding abilities to peak, and that would be great against the Demons. Also a hell of an insult to them."

Miles could figure how that would be quite a spiteful card to play. "So where is the Karma Scale, then?"

"Kalivan Tor, last I heard."

Miles remembered that planet's name from when he visited Zharekk. The solar system known as The Strife Planets had three habitable worlds in orbit of its parent star: Zharekk, Raon-Arashal, and Kalivan Tor. But the idea that Jaden *heard* the Scale was on Kalivan Tor was odd, since that was the planet that had by far the least dealings with the rest of the universe, given that the Vulpian population, known as Siivalar Vulpians were exceptionally reclusive.

"How did you manage to hear that it's probably on Kalivan Tor?" Miles questioned.

"The Siivalar Vulpians and other scattered species on that planet have few dealings with the universe, not none."

Miles figured he wasn't going to get a helpful answer out of Jaden anytime soon, and that it was best to not bother from there. After agreeing to help and closing the channel, Miles couldn't help but feel uneasy with the idea of heading to Kalivan Tor. He couldn't pinpoint why, but something about that planet just seemed... off. It had the shortest orbital path of the three Strife Planets, and was incredibly hot on the surface, so the entirety of civilization existed underground there. But that wasn't what put him on edge. He just figured something else was fundamentally not right with the planet.

"I don't know why," Miles said to the Effigy after summoning it. "Kalivan Tor just seems like... something is about to happen there. Something bad, I can't shake it."

The effigy sat in silence, as always.

"That won't stop me from going there. Quite the opposite, in fact. I think I need to head there more than before, when Jaden was explaining the Karma Scale's deal."

Miles's next questions were for the Aura Prism, as he soon found himself visiting The Mountain and its peak.

"You are not alone in your unease towards Kalivan Tor," the Prism affirmed, but that didn't comfort. "I too sense something foul on that planet, something gnaws at the children of Old Cynofrax there, the Siivalar Vulpians. I don't know if this is the work of Demons or their masters, but it would not be beyond possibility."

"Xenidar told me a while back that with The Aura, it's an even worse idea than usual to ignore the goosebumps and hairs standing on end. That instincts become a lot less wrong when psionically boosted in reliability."

"And he is right to say that."

A moment passed as Miles pondered, and the Prism likely was as well. There wasn't any way to tell, though, given that the Aura Prism was a Prism, and didn't exactly emote.

"I do hope you plan to make for Kalivan Tor. As for Jaden's request of the Karma Scale... I would've been worried if she wanted to use it. But I suppose it'd be a very Jaden thing to want such an artifact for a completely different reason than the artifact itself."

"I mean, I'll start off looking for the Scale," Miles determined "But I get the feeling that it'll take a back seat before too long."

The rest of that day was spent on preparations. Miles figured he was going to be on Kalivan Tor for a while, and would need to be able to 'rough it' for a bit before the end. Within the Aura Runner, he packed his Cutlass, the Borfblade, and his ranged weapons, as much as he wasn't fond of admitting he'd probably need them. The Orvitarian Collapse Rifle and AZP-621 Multi-Munition

Pistol, with ammo to spare. Not an enormous amount, he wanted to travel decently light. Even though The Aura made him able to not need sleep, and rarely need food, he loaded some survival rations into the Aura Runner's cargo hold, as 'rarely' still wasn't 'never.'

Miles figured with the supplies he was bringing, five ASC (a little under sixteen Earth years) underground easily. As long as his mind could take it. As much as he figured he was mentally stronger than most Humans, Miles still knew that no Human society had ever successfully lived underground, given the inherent psychological disposition to discomfort and eventual madness if there aren't any plants or sunlight around.

"Fuckin' monkey-brain bullshit," Miles muttered to himself as he remembered that very fact. His tone soon switched to a mocking one. "Ooh, look at me, I'm psychologically hardwired to go insane if I don't see plants for enough time! So sensitive and delicate am I, that I need to see the sun or it's ooooover!"

This grumbling continued for some time.

"All right then, Kalivan Tor," Miles finally told himself after getting over his rant on the limitations of the mortal form. Even when The Aura assured time could not kill him, Miles still seemed to have plenty of complaints about fragile Human bodies all the same. Fortunately, this story does not take place before he

<GREGOR FJELLREV>

gained his power, or one would hear a lot more of that.

The Aura Runner touched down on the barren surface of Kalivan Tor, an outside heat warning flashing on the screen. Miles had brought the Personal Defense Grid Generator, which would also act as a hostile environment shield, letting him stand without burning, and breathe without choking. Miles stepped out of the ship after activating said Defense Grid and grabbing his cutlass, then turned on his scanner.

But something made the scanner go awry. Some kind of interference made it utterly unusable, which should have been impossible, right?

"Everyone's underground," Miles remembered. "And I'm willing to bet they prefer psionics to electronics."

Shaking off the rhyme, Miles concentrated, letting The Aura act as a new set of eyes, which turned his natural ones a glowing gold-amber color. Psionics indeed, and deep beneath the surface of the planet. But there seemed to be no entrances or shafts at ground level.

"Then how does one get down there?" Miles wondered aloud, looking for some kind of hint or clue.

He found one in a trail of energy that he followed for a few minutes, and ended with a circle of that same faint trace of power. Standing in its center, Miles jolted

<FIRE TO BURN THE STARS>

his hand upwards slightly, causing a sudden shift in the crusted and cracked dirt. The ground began to turn and spin, and soon form a staircase downwards, into the planet.

"I'll take it."

Descending this staircase, it only went down fifty or so feet before ending at a natural cavern of some kind, and sealing itself back up. But the temperature was still too hot for Miles to not burn if he didn't have the Defense Grid.

"Well, that doesn't make a whole lot of sense," he said before refocusing The Aura's sight. The place was pitch-black otherwise, and he was able to make it look as though there was ambient light, at least. Not bright, but definitely discernible.

The tunnels weren't cramped, but there wasn't much space between Miles's head and the hard dirt ceiling that was more like sandstone at this depth.

Hours passed as he walked and followed the faint trace of old Psionic energy. Not even ancient, or primordial... but 'old' was the term he would call it by. Not quite obsolete, but stretched long past what one would think its lifespan could normally be, like a Civic from the 90's, borderline immortal, until the instant it stopped proving so.

Miles soon found boroughs carved from the

sandstone walls, little neighborhoods of homes built from the underground's solidity and shelter. But these wouldn't have acted sufficiently as shelter at this depth, the Defense Grid was still blocking otherwise lethal temperatures.

"Maybe the planet was drifting towards the star? Or the star expanded?" Miles hypothesized. "But they're still around, just deeper. I suppose I'll get to ask them soon enough."

Suddenly, though, the almost-cramped tunnel opened up into an enormous maw of a subterranean city, carved from the sandstone of the great cavern it rested in.

"I think I can camp here for a bit, call it a hunch," he eventually said after a solid minute or two of silent wonder and admiration. The cities of Cynofrax were one thing, the Spire of Turazin the Conclave met in and the temple-like Hideout were another, but this was a new level for some reason to him. Perhaps it was the fact that all those cities were on the surface, but this wasn't. More likely he also had this understanding that this was a city clawed from the hostility of its own foundations, a planet battered by scorching sun and no doubt terrifying underground beasts of old. That despite all that, this was a city that stood so stalwart all the same. The depth was almost survivable, according to the actual module that projected his shield. Maybe a species from this planet could do it naturally. But there were no lifeforms nearby, so Miles summoned the Effigy after setting up a small camp to take a break at.

"I almost might consider this my first 'field mission,' so to speak," he started. "I mean, Avanchenvaldr was a duel to get my feet wet, Hulae was a fight of attrition I didn't anticipate, even the Opponent Unbeatable, that was just a loose end being tied. Killentarn was a decision in a split second. But this... this is something else for sure."

Still listening as ever, the effigy sat with Miles, and so Miles continued.

"I suppose you're more than just who I'd be if I was better. You're what I'd want in my ally. Well, not even just ally. More than that. The next step, I never found the word for. I never could use the ones my language had, they were all so sappy and insipid. I always figured I'll have to make my own that means 'ultimate ally.'"

Miles thought for a moment, wondering if he could suddenly get that word now, but to no avail.

"A friend and comrade you would be proud to say you stand with, who you'd without a moment's hesitation fight back-to-back alongside unto the end of time itself, because you know, you understand they'd do the same, even if never you needed to tell each other. You could trust them with your darkest and most damning secrets, but you'd never need to. A respect unparalleled, and your aims align to aid each other."

Miles even smiled a little, as if he were fantasizing about being next to that kind of person right now.

"What would that word be? What could you call that person? That... ultimate ally? It's the mystery we've pondered our whole lives."

He truly couldn't think of a word befitting such a wondrous companion. No word he knew could do it justice. He really would have to make one of his own.

"Regardless, that is not the mystery I need to be solving today."

Miles stayed at his little camp for a few hours, admiring the grand hall he sat inside, wondering why this city would be abandoned, even if it was getting to hot to handle. Why would the people here give up on a place like this and leave it to gather dust? He couldn't even call it ruins, because it was old and abandoned, but far from ruined by any stretch. The emptiness seemed even more so than it should, and Miles soon figured out why: It was just the stonework that remained. No furniture even made from stone, the tables and chairs in houses gone while the slabwork bedframes remained. The essence of a ghost town.

It wasn't as unnerving as it was alerting. Miles didn't fear for what may have emptied this place, but he did keep himself sharp more than he had before. Further into the tunnels, his Defense Grid Generator pinged. He had passed beyond the thermal protection threshold, so he switched it off to save its power, letting The Aura's passive enhancements keep him able to breathe in an atmosphere he might normally not be able to.

Using The Aura's sight once again, Miles looked deep below where the population clusters were. Other than scattered insects and the like, he was alone down here.

No, wait, he wasn't.

The Sight alerted Miles to a new presence, less than a hundred feet away, and hiding. Whatever this thing was, it was using its own power to make it impossible to pinpoint, but there was no mistaking its presence's existence. Miles turned around, facing back down the tunnel, that had several offshoots too small for him to crawl through.

"Whoever's there, I know that you're out here. There's no need to hide from me, I come as an ally, sent by the Aura Prism of Cynofrax. And Jaden of Laksor, I suppose. She just wanted the Elurian Karma Scale, pick your favorite, I guess…"

From about fifty feet back, a small Vulpian

tentatively revealed himself. Not as short as Xenidar or other Talvas Vulpians, but whoever he was, he certainly wasn't imposing.

"You... you make a strange-odd request," the creature he understood was a Siivalar Vulpian said, in a unique sort of slang-dialect. "Two of them? Between the Karma Scale and the Prism-bidding?"

"Honestly, the Karma Scale can take a backseat if it needs to. The Aura Prism told me that the Siivalar, which I assume you are of?" The Vulpian nodded at Miles's pause for confirmation. "The Prism told me the Siivalar could use aid of some kind, couldn't pinpoint what and neither could I. But the Prism did understand that something was needed by the Vulpians of Kalivan Tor."

The mentions of the Aura Prism, and Miles's knowledge of the planet's name and that of its dominant species seemed to give this Siivalar some comfort, who approached slightly closer. Still a good twenty feet away overall, though. "I'm... Tviri," he finally introduced himself. "You can fate-defend?"

"I'm Miles Radien, and if that's what is needed, it's what I've come here to do."

Tviri seemed nervous. Not because of what he was about to say and whether or not he should say it, but more afraid of what may very well be the reason he may have hoped or prayed for a hero.

"The Siivalar. All of Kalivan Tor..., it's error-living. Wrong-existing. I can't seem to find the word..."

"Well, join the club." Miles remarked, relating to the Siivalar's plight of diction.

"Club for word-failing?" Tviri asked, almost offended but more confused.

"Sorry, it's an expression. A... not-literal? Speech-figure-construct?" Miles quickly attempted to rectify, though tripping up a little on how to explain the word 'metaphor.' Even so, Tviri seemed to figure it out, nodding as he at least understood the overall message. "Even so," Miles continued "What's going on here that's got you this unnerved?"

"There are so few visitors or outsiders who come to Kalivan Tor. But not even that. That isn't the problem-fear. The Siivalar power... our power as Vulpian... it's old-fading. We've stretched this... unworking energy far beyond its life-effective."

"Go on," Miles encouraged.

"Burst-Type Psionics, we Siivalar are. Long, long ago there were power-styles, before people came to know all power as one-source. Burst-Type meant our power was limited, but fast-potent. We could... we still only let loose mass amounts of power over instant-time, needing long breaks before bursting again."

Miles listened, at the very least understanding what was going on, odd conjugations and all.

"Burst-Type is long since irrelevant," Tviri continued. "But it's who we are. And it is fading away."

"One can only recharge a battery so many times," Miles added.

"Yes! Exactly!" Tviri affirmed, a little excited that Miles gave him the words he was looking for. "We've tried to find something else. A different way to power-wield. But the problem is, with all power being from one-source, the problem is with the Siivalar."

Tviri almost seemed ashamed at that understanding.

"And is there a reason the Siivalar do not leave Kalivan Tor?" Miles asked. "You and your kind are recognized as Vulpian, are you not? Shouldn't you be able to find haven on Vulpian worlds?"

Tviri shook his head. "The Siivalar have become weak compared to the rest of power-wielders. We couldn't last. Not with this weakened-old Psi…"

Miles sighed. Not out of frustration for Tviri countering his suggestion, but more for the fact that Tviri was probably right. In a universe long since moved on from the Burst-Type Psionic 'style,' a species exclusively of that kind would likely be shunned and even attacked for it.

"Maybe there's something I can do," Miles said. "There has to be a way to aid the Siivalar, and I'll help find it out."

Tviri looked to Miles and nodded, motioning for him to follow. Not far from where they found each other, there was a sort of Gravity Shaft leading to where the Siivalar were living, not far from Kalivan Tor's mantle, that they could float down and disembark after a few minutes, which they did. Miles's landing was almost a little rough, but he managed to salvage it. Tviri continued to lead through the Siivalar settlements, and though Miles received rather odd looks from other Siivalar, they were more the kind of hopeful odd. That maybe whoever was walking among them could be the key to their survival, at least for now.

"Not far now," Tviri said, entering a side passage of some kind. Miles followed, and soon found himself in a much larger chamber lit by a blue font of energy that acted like a Psionically-powered fire. Every now and then, a Siivalar would approach this font and unleash a rapid burst of power to keep it fueled, then head back to whatever they were doing before to recover until they next needed to put energy into the font.

"This is one of the Core-Fonts," Tviri explained. "A network all across the under-tunnels we power-burst into, to keep the world alive, and power the under-towns."

It didn't even take using the Sight to see that it only had so much life left in it, and only so many more times it could be refueled before even that failed. Miles raised his hand towards the font, but Tviri stopped him.

"Not what you're here for," Tviri assured, leading Miles further in to a different chamber, where there appeared to be some kind of leadership meeting.

"Leaders, this is Miles Radien," Tviri opened with, bringing the Siivalar within this chamber to silence. It seemed as though they hadn't seen someone from outside Kalivan Tor their whole lives. "He offers aid, at the bidding of the Prism."

Miles seemed to notice Tviri had been using less of his odd little conjugations, but it was possible that The Aura's translating ability for him was getting more intuitive as it heard the language that likely hadn't been heard outside this planet for a very long time.

Many of the 'leaders' seemed uneasy at the mention of the Prism. "The Prism? Why would Cynofrax only send aid now, at the eve of our fading?" one asked, turning to Miles with a look of impatience.

"The Prism was not the first being that told me I should come to Kalivan Tor," Miles explained. "But the Prism certainly said it was a good idea. Tviri has made me aware of the Siivalar's situation. Your power is fading, and you don't trust the universe to not take advantage of the fact you still have to rely on Burst-Type power-wielding."

This was met with muttering and annoyance.

"Frankly, I don't blame you for that," Miles added. "If my home world taught me anything, it's that there's plenty of people out there who love little more than to take what excuse they can get, and just ride that advantage for decades if they can."

There was still plenty of muttering, but less annoyance overall.

"I also should say the Prism isn't omniscient, and that the Siivalar are secluded as all hell, so it wouldn't be easy to notice that help was needed given that no one was asking, as far as I know. But I do understand the hesitation towards asking."

"Regardless, what would you have us do?" a Siivalar leader asked. "The fact remains that our time in the universe is ending, and we would rather it didn't."

"I don't know how to help you, but I want to. If there's something that can give me an answer here on Kalivan Tor, I would invite it to make itself known. The mere fact that the Siivalar have lasted this long on so little stands as testimony to your hardiness and resilience. I've little doubt the universe could use people like that. Besides, Psionic power isn't the only thing that matters. Your cousins on Talvakorrik almost forsake power entirely in favor of—"

"The Talvas preference to engineering does not concern us!" an older leader shouted, but was quickly hushed by his comrades.

"Seems the elderly rarely change, regardless of species," Miles commented before continuing. "The Siivalar can yet have a place, if only just a different planet for now. But before I can really offer solutions, I need to know more about the problem. I know that your power is fading and all, that Kalivan Tor isn't as sustainable as it once was, but I need to know more *on* that. Is there somewhere I can learn perhaps *why* it's all dying?"

This was met by silence, and exchanged glances, as though the Siivalar were telepathically debating amongst themselves whether or not to reveal the nature of their dying power to this outsider. It was rather likely that was exactly what they were doing.

"If a definite answer exists, if there is something beyond what we know of this, the answers will be in the Torgaen Fields," one of the Siivalar finally spoke. A few others looked to her oddly, as if she had just said something they agreed not to mention. This didn't stop her, though. "Tviri will guide you there, and gods willing, you may be able to do something of it."

"Of course," Tviri acknowledged. "Radien, we must be swift-paced!"

<FIRE TO BURN THE STARS>

"Aye!" Miles agreed, following Tviri out of the council chambers.

The rest of the day was spent traveling towards these Torgaen Fields, and according to Tviri, this was where most of the Siivalar's knowledge was kept, in a huge natural chamber within the underground stored in Psionic memory holograms. If there was an answer to the Siivalar plight, it would be there.

"Tviri, while my priority is with helping your people, do you happen to know where the Elurian Karma Scale is?" Miles asked.

Tviri thought for a moment, then nodded. "That can be aid-payment." Miles figured it was fair. Perhaps even Jaden's GAMA, if the enhancements from the blood on the Scale worked, could help the Siivalar. Eventually, the two stopped in another one of the abandoned boroughs to take a break. Tviri produced a bottle from his pack, offering some of it's contents to Miles after taking a swig himself. It tasted like cheap ale, but it was likely the best the species could do in the conditions. A product of its situation, that did quite well for it, much like the Katana sword. And like the Katana, someone definitely could ruin this ale for everyone else by being really weird about their insistence that it was the greatest ever.

"Tviri?" Miles got the attention of his guide. "I

wonder if you have a word for something I can't seem to find one for."

Tviri turned and soon tilted his head a little. "A word? I thought we were in the club of word-failing," he said jokingly, to Miles's surprise and subsequent almost spitting out of the drink they were sharing.

"Cheeky bugger, you!" Miles finally said, and the two laughed. "But seriously, I do wonder if your people, your languages have a word that I can't seem to find."

Tviri took a decent glug of drink before saying he'd try.

"The ultimate ally," Miles explained. "Someone you'd be proud to stand alongside, back-to-back unto the end of time itself, because you know they'd do the same. You could trust this ally with your darkest and most damning secrets, but you know you'd never actually have to. A respect unmatched, paramount between you and this ultimate ally. Truly, a being who defies all the odds just by existing, let alone existing alongside you. The one who could make you say you stand united instead of alone…"

As Miles explained, Tviri seemed to relate. Not necessarily to what he was talking about, but to the idea. The ultimate ally, it seemed to resonate with Tviri. After a moment, he spoke.

"I know what you're talking about, I do," Tviri

said. "But I don't have a word either. I don't think any words fit."

"Aye, I always felt the same," Miles responded, leaning against the wall in the small sandstone hovel they rested in.

"That... ultimate-ally... I think you'd understand when you knew them, if that makes sense." The way Tviri said the word 'understand,' he enunciated it just like some of the other pseudo-slang words he used, like 'understand' was slang itself. "Not when you saw them, gods no. But you could know that person... you could know that ally when they knew you."

"I think I get it," Miles commented. "But I'm at least relieved to see that I'm not the only one who's wondered about this sort of thing."

"You couldn't seek this word," Tviri also said. "I... I can know that for sure. You can't go looking for the person who this word is. It would never work."

Miles nodded. "Aye, no doubt. I even doubt that you could even make it known you're wanting of something like that ultimate ally. Y'know how... if enough unsavory types knew you were looking for this ultimate ally, it could make it all the easier to pose as one, and become a parasite of your very soul."

Tviri nodded this time, and the two sat in silence after that for a bit. Nothing more really needed to be said, nothing that would add anything useful, at least. They sat there for several hours, it seemed, just taking a break from needing to do anything. Tviri stood up first, eventually.

"Torgaen fields aren't exactly sick-distance to begin with, so we're pretty close now."

Miles seemed to understand that 'sick-distance' meant something along the lines of 'obnoxiously distant,' where it's the sort of length that isn't too far if you're sort of 'autopilot walking,' but that definitely feels infinite if you're consciously aware of how far you have yet to go before finally reaching the steps of your home. Regardless, they pressed forth.

Tviri struck up a conversation to induce that autopilot walking that would make the trip feel shorter, asking Miles if he had heard of a few different things, certain legends of the stars, and some of their treasures, from the classic to the oddball. The Box of Spatial Distortion certainly sounded interesting. Apparently, it was created by Felinian scientists hoping to solve the universe's very specific problem of not finding the right sized box for things, but the instructions to create them had to be destroyed, since more often than not, Felinians, and also Taigron, Lysanarr, and Hajivakk would prefer to just sit within these boxes that automatically resized themselves to perfectly fit whatever occupied them. As a result, several industrial worlds had their economies brought to utter ruin as a result of "Box-sitting addiction", unique to feline species of the stars, and some Draconians.

Other legends like that of the Honorblade of Korvideyl, the Kendradeyne Code and the Eye of Akoraveon filled the time until Tviri noted they had reached the Torgaen Fields.

"We're here. The memory-fields of Torgaen."

"Was Torgaen a person or something? A Siivalar of note?" Miles inquired.

"No, he was Haji-Son. T'Sen Torgaen, longest-living of the Defenders. Though... who is the Defender now?"

Miles stopped as he remembered that there was no Defender right now. Caltoran had been killed not long ago in the manner he had died, and there did not currently exist such a person by that title.

"I don't think... anyone right now," Miles said. "A Laksorian named Caltoran held that title, but was killed rather recently. I suppose the worlds are in the lull period between him and the next one, assuming there will be a next one."

"There is always a Defender," Tviri corrected. "For as long as life has lived, there has been a Defender. The last breath of a Defender is the first breath of their successor. But with Caltoran's death... yes, the worlds would be yet-waiting for the next to be known."

"That aside, this is the place we can find answers?" Miles asked, to which Tviri nodded. Stepping forward, Miles soon found himself wandering this underground cavern, not realizing it had become a grassy knoll until he noticed as well, a wispy fog at eye level, not so thick that he couldn't see through, not even all that obstructing. But the terrain had changed indeed.

Miles suddenly heard movement, and gripped his cutlass that had been with him since his arrival on the planet. But what passed by him was a spectre of some kind, a faint silhouette of an ancient warrior charging at an unseen foe. Unseen, that was, until the spectre leaped forward with a snapping front kick, knocking down the shadow of an enemy that only just became visible.

Both then disappeared.

A different set of shadows now simply seemed to converse with each other before fading. Another shade stood in front of some kind of altar. But there was nothing to discern from this. Miles couldn't see anything that he might be looking for.

"All right, what does this look like?" Miles started turning the gears in his head. By now, a few other sets of spectres had come and gone, but then the one kicking down his opponent returned, followed by another he had seen previously, but further down the line than last time. "A pseudo-puzzle in an RPG. So the solution is simple: Find the order. What happened when. Then something useful will come of it."

Miles then realized that it wasn't the order that was altered, it was the location he stood in. The shadow with the kick, it was always in one spot. The single person sitting in a corner at a fire as he lamented, same situation. On the ground were metal wedges, and there was his key.

"If I know my pseudo-puzzles for the purpose of advancing plot, I just need to find the order, and assemble the wheel."

Seven wedges with pictograms of seven events. Miles laid them out on a stone table that... wasn't there before. Miles figured that the place to put the wedges was in the table, and sure enough, a circle was carved out of the center, perfectly sized to fit the complete wheel.

"All right, let's figure this out. A warrior push kicks his opponent, someone laments at a fire, two people converse, someone stands at an altar, a person pleads at... wait, these things have stuff on the reverse side, that might help."

Studying the carvings on the tail sides of each wedge, they did offer a little help. Words that likely formed a story.

"Okay, this helps a bit. The warrior kicking someone, 'Desperately, he may yet break the cycle.' The two in conversation, 'Youthfully, he forges his allies.' The guy pleading to a parliament-looking thing, 'Knowingly, he assures the better way.' This guy atop a mound of bodies. 'Furiously, he brings to ruin.' Guy at an altar, 'Painfully, his cruel understanding.' Guy with his sword held high, 'Miraculously, he finds a better way.' As for being moody at the fire..."

Miles's heart skipped a beat as he read it.

"He stands alone."

A moment passed as he deciphered this prophecy.

"Those are my words. Radien stands alone."

Miles swiftly arranged the pieces.

"Youthfully, he forges his allies. Painfully, his cruel understanding. Miraculously, he finds a better way. Desperately, he may yet break the cycle. Knowingly, he assures the better way. Furiously, he brings to ruin. He stands alone."

The table shifted, and Miles felt a gust of wind hit him as the fog coalesced into a being.

"T'Sen Torgaen?" Miles asked.

"I am far from even the shadow of T'Sen," the being responded. "Nor was I put here by him. But I assume you understand that is irrelevant."

"Then tell me what is."

"You can tell where you stand on that wheel, and I will not tire you with promises of vagueness that are the nature of prophecy. But that vagueness may be what saves you, what saves this world. That prophecy does not need to be for you."

The impatience in Miles's face was unmistakable.

"Return to the Siivalar conclave. Tell them the way you have planned to ensure their place in the worlds, and spare no haste, for the plans of the oldest foes are meant to last beyond the lifetimes of stars."

"I don't have a plan yet, but I guess I'll have to think of something along the way," Miles figured.

The being in the fog stepped aside, letting Miles begin his rush back to the Siivalar city. But what unnerved him most was that Tviri had left him, likely heading back himself.

"Wait, holy shit, I do have a plan now! And it honestly might actually work!" Miles said to himself as he ran some ideas through his head on his way back to Siivalar territory.

Finally reaching his destination, Miles sprinted towards the conclave chambers. Along the way, seeing a single Siivalar Vulpian approaching the font in the town. Miles fired a bolt at the font to charge it, yelling 'You're good!' as he made his way past.

A few others came to the font to verify. "He's...

actually right. This thing's been charged for a good month's worth!" one finally confirmed, to the relief and celebratory sighs of the locals.

When he approached the entrance to the conclave's chambers, Miles saw a single guard there, blocking the closed door.

"The conclave is in session right now, no one is to enter," this guard said, to Miles's confusion.

"What are you on about?! I'm back, I have the plan to save the Siivalar!" Miles protested.

"The plan for Kalivan Tor and its people is what the conclave are discussing right now, and I am sure they will be open to suggestion once they have concluded this meeting," the guard continued in a rather rehearsed manner, as if he'd had to say that several times already from a cue card.

"What?! No! Your conclave sent *me* to the Torgaen Fields to *find* the solution, and I have that now!"

"Look, if you have a suggestion of your own, I am positive the conclave would hear it. Until then, they must not be disturbed. Please, move on."

Miles turned around in frustration, gripping his hair before essentially deciding to hell with it, charging forward and inevitably leaping forward with a kick that sent the Siivalar guard crashing through the door to the chambers, which Miles then promptly rushed into.

"What in all creation is the meaning of this interruption?!" one of the leaders yelled.

Miles looked around the room for a split second before starting his piece, noticing the conclave, what appeared to be a diplomat from one of the felinoid species of the universe, the Lysanarr, and Tviri, who definitely would have some explaining to do.

"Tviri, you definitely will have some explaining to do," Miles affirmed. "I'm not sure why you lot have convened to discuss a plan for Kalivan Tor when I still hadn't yet returned from the Torgaen Fields with an answer, which I now have, by the way!"

"Your expedition to Torgaen Fields was entirely your own will, prompted by a single one of us, who is no longer in service. She did not speak for the will of the conclave as a whole."

"Well, clearly she should've been, since she had more brains than all of you! And who's this Lysanarr here? Why was I not made aware of his presence, he's clearly been here a while judging by the dirt on his pants!"

The Lysanarr actually then checked his pants, which sure enough, had a fair amount of dust-turned-dirt on them from casual walking about in the tunnels for months.

"My name is Valras, I'm here on behalf of the

Lysanarr Parliament of Gelvetori, to make sure that the Siivalar people of—"

Miles's eyes flashed golden yellow as he used The Aura's sight to discern what information was needed. Finding it, he turned back to the leaders of Kalivan Tor.

"Bullshit you're a diplomat, you've got Dark Six energy crawling all over you! Can none of you guys see it on him? It's damn near seething!"

"Without the ability to rely on Psionic power to attain that kind of information, such as it is, we must reach our conclusion by the facts on hand," a conclave member spoke up. "Those facts are that Valras has been here arranging Kalivan Tor's re-integration into the universe for several months, and you have only just recently shown up here, with a rather volatile demeanor."

"Several months?! Why did no one tell me?! Tviri, why didn't *you* tell me?!"

Silence followed, clearly Miles wasn't getting an answer.

"Besides, what's this jackass's plan to get you back in the universe? Lemme guess, some kind of oath written in a language that you don't recognize, but this dude assures you is some primordial tongue, spoken by gods or whatever the fuck he wants you to figure, that'll make an accord with some divine champion to give

Siivalar power a patch update of sorts? Because if that's the plan, that's a pretty sad attempt at subtlety! I'd bet a lifetime supply of… whatever; that the words in some dead language are a pledge to the Dark Six, and they'll hold every one of you to it, even if you don't know what you're doing, because *I mean, you technically said the words so that's good enough!* Then someone's gotta make the tough call to put you down, and I should know!"

A silence that was somehow even more silent than the previous one followed.

"Oh, for fuck's sake, *please* tell me that wasn't right! That was supposed to be the ridiculous guess that there's no way could've been accurate!"

Suddenly, Miles felt a jolting pain in his leg. The guard he kicked through the door had worked up the strength to stab him there, and he yelped and cursed as he turned to the guard but was blasted by the Lysanarr unconscious. Though wounded, the guard managed to stand himself up.

"The conclave thanks you for your willingness to your duty, even when wounded, guardsman Virkii. Take the time you need to heal," a leader noted, to agreement from the rest.

"Unfortunately, killing this one would not aid us at all," the Lysanarr noted. "If the Prism indeed sent him, then it is keeping watch. Not completely vigilant, but certainly enough to know the instant if he were to die."

Miles woke up in a scrapcobble prison cell, clearly constructed not long ago to house someone quickly, but reliably. Groaning and cursing a few times, he did also comment that he'd had worse hangovers.

"Don't worry, they didn't construct it just for you," a voice said behind him. Turning around, Miles saw a Laksorian in the dark corner, where it was cooler. They were near to the core of the planet, and it was quite hot. Though Miles's Defense Grid generator was gone, passive use of The Aura made sure he didn't burn, but he still was sweating. The Laksorian likely relied on some power of his own as well. "They constructed it just for me at first."

"I guess they don't have other prisons?" Miles questioned.

"Not till a Laksorian started getting too close for comfort by coincidence." He then stood up to introduce himself. "Revek of Laksor. And you are?"

"Miles Radien. I know a scientist from Laksor."

"Wouldn't happen to be a specialist in Genome Hacking?"

"The very same. I assume you're the lab assistant she mentioned when she asked me to head over here?"

"Aye. I was only after the Elurian Karma Scale, and

<FIRE TO BURN THE STARS>

just so happened to notice that something malicious was turning the gears of Kalivan Tor, and that malicious thing had unfortunately gained the trust of the Siivalar, so it was my word against his, which wasn't too much help."

Miles sighed with mutual annoyance to this. "As nice as it would be, griping about the sheer obnoxiousness of our situation won't help. What is even with all this tech at the core? Aren't they funneling power into the fonts, rather than keeping the core alive through technology?"

"Yes, and no," Revek replied, standing up and next to Miles. "All the tech and power are here, working on some... thing. It looks like an energy amplifier of some kind, and the Siivalar are charging it with their bursts, with very little left over to sustain the actual life going on. But I can't tell for sure, I'm not Jaden."

"You don't sound like a dunce, though."

"She only says that because my area is fieldwork, and the non-booksmarts that are required for it. But she knows we've each got our specialties. If she were trying to attain information through normal, non-interrogative conversation, I'd be the one calling her a dunce."

"Either way, we need to figure something out, if only just getting out of this cell."

Revek laughed. "Oh, way ahead of you. I've been in and out multiple times, putting the cage back together before the patrols and check-ins. All the tech might be here, but the Siivalar power is still old and dying."

"Fair enough. I'll let you take the lead for the parts you already know."

Revek nodded. "And we should figure out what questions need to be answered, in what priority."

Miles nodded this time. "In unprioritized order, we need to know what this machine is, what it's end goal is, where that damn Lysanarr's at, what plans he has to what end, how to save the Siivalar, and the one I will prioritize as last, getting the Karma Scale."

"I agree. The Scale can sure as hell wait. With the core machine here, let's figure it out first, and from that, we can extrapolate the priority of the Siivalar and their respective needs."

Revek lifted the gate off of its hinges and set it aside. "One hour until the check-in patrol gets within eyeshot of the cell, leaves fifty minutes to figure this out, minus any amount of time spent getting to a given point in the structure, for the route back."

"Works for me. Have you found an interface device here?"

Revek showed Miles to the controls themselves, noting that the language they were written in was too old for him to recognize. Miles also had some trouble with it, because it looked like a hybrid of at least two languages mashed together and hit with a hammer.

"I can barely get it, The Aura's having a tough time with the hybridization of what's honestly probably the Siivalar written language and a form of Demonic."

Revek suddenly looked like a light bulb went off in his head. "Demonic! That's the other one! Now I can see it, hell."

"Did... did you not pick up the Dark Six energy the Lysanarr was basically bleeding from every orifice?"

"No, because I didn't have the time to scan him before he convinced them to chuck me in here and confiscate my shit!"

Miles remembered that not everyone non-human was a power-wielder. "Right, so now we both know that the Dark Six are the ones behind this. Does that turn on any more light bulbs?"

Revek seemed a little confused at the metaphor.

"Oh my goodness, does that give us any more answers?" Miles also remembered that light bulbs were basically an Earth thing, and bulbs of electric light had been phased out of technological relevance long ago for the universe. At least, bulb-shaped lights.

"Yeah... Now that I know it's Dark Six, it does." Revek looked up and down at the machine they stood in the guts of, fitting the pieces together and clearly not liking the implications of the result. "It's a fucking planet-

<GREGOR FJELLREV>

scale Deoxian Pulse Engine!"

Miles stood there. "I'm sure some day I'll be in your shoes when I ask you today to explain what the hell that is."

"Deoxian Pulses are waves of energy tailored to specific DNA sequences. Basically, the point is to send a wave of... whatever that only affects a given species. They're staggeringly illegal as weapons, and highly regulated as medical devices. Y'know, trying to heal a whole planet of wounded? That's what they're *supposed* to do," Revek explained, putting aside any frustration of Miles's lack of knowledge on planetary technologies. Looking at some of the readouts on screen, Revek's tone became much more urgent. "It's equipped with an energy converter to turn the power that locals are funneling to it into Dark Six energy! And with the Deoxian Pulse set to Siivalar DNA..."

"It's going to turn every single one of them into Dark Six servants," Miles finished, the gears clicking into place for him now. "Every Siivalar, controlled by the Dark Six, and now wielding their power, the Lords of Evil get a whole species as an army, behind the Barriers, and able to summon rifts with that power!"

"Every Siivalar, a rift generator," Revek continued. "Ten Siivalar to a planet at most, and even just a hundred on Cynofrax could take the planet and destroy the Aura Prism. They probably don't even know this is where their power goes."

"The hell do we do then? We can't overload and blow it, at least, not as long as the Siivalar aren't aware of what's going on! And that Lysanarr has their ear, there's gotta be something!"

"The Lysanarr would be my bet," Revek suggested. "Take him out, and at the very least the poison stops flowing, however much remains in the system."

A clang was heard as a door started being opened, getting the attention of the duo. After exchanging glances that said, *That wasn't even thirty minutes!*, they decided that they needed to make their move now. At least there were two of them.

The pair of guards that entered, however, were not as dynamic of a duo, and were quickly incapacitated not long after leaving the elevator. When it arrived at the mantle region, Miles stepped out, conjuring the Chronokey for the Aura Runner in his hand. The one thing the Siivalar couldn't confiscate, since it, like the ship it was for, was in a Temporal Displacement by Miles's will.

"Get to Zharekk, contact Moldrenor. I've done work with him on behalf of Jaden before. My ship is on the surface," Miles instructed. "Gods willing, you can get backup."

Revek nodded, taking the Chronokey and heading off with haste towards one of the routes to the surface. Miles knew what needed to be done, but not how to proceed afterwards. The Lysanarr Valras had to die, but the Siivalar wouldn't take kindly to that. The best plan he had was to take him out, then secure the Deoxian Pulse Engine to prevent its use until he could think of something better.

The Aura's Sight allowed Miles to quickly pinpoint where Valras was, he didn't even have to trace him specifically, just where the Dark Six energy was coming from. Quite conveniently, the Dark Six energy was originating from the same place his stuff was. Specifically, his cutlass, the Borfblade. The trace of the Red Dust that the Borfblade had made it possible to discern where it was being kept, some kind of... private armory? It wasn't where the guard armory was, nor just sitting in someone's home. Valras may very well have taken it for himself at some point.

However, as he was planning and tracing this route, a Siivalar noticed him, and started to skitter off to alert the rest. Miles heard the claws on stone, and used The Aura to halt the fleeing cur in his place, and drag him over, who stood frozen in fear.

Miles considered killing him. He really did. This was a scout, one of the patrolling Siivalar from the outskirts of the cities, and Miles at first knew he couldn't let this guy live. But even though he had used The Aura to stop this Siivalar from setting off an alarm, it took him a second to remember that he had The Aura's power, and could use it for things other than combat.

A quick motion of the hand, and the Siivalar fainted. The Aura next made sure he'd have no memory of noticing Miles when he woke up in a few minutes, and so he continued on his route towards his sword, and his Defense Grid Generator.

Valras had indeed taken Miles's gear into where he was staying, one of the sandstone houses that looked like any other. Likely part of the plan from his Demonic masters, as making sure he had lavish living conditions would be a bit of a dead giveaway, especially on a dying world like Kalivan Tor. The Dark Six were evil, but they were clever, intuitive, understanding of the people they were trying to conquer and destroy. They knew how things worked, and how to use that to disguise themselves and their presence.

However, the Defense Grid Generator was broken, smashed into pieces for the scraps of technology within. The battery's power alone could probably charge one of the town fonts for a year. The Borfblade, however, was where Miles saw it in The Aura's Sight, and the air around it had a slightly... charred scent. Like something burned very hot and very fast. Was someone testing the durability of the Borfblade?

Miles took ahold of it, unsheathing it, and soon discovering just what happened, with the aid of the Sight. Apparently, the exposure to raw power that the Borfblade had channeled, both in training and combat, had allowed it to gain the ability to recognize its correct wielder, and someone else had tried to test it out before he came along. It didn't end well for the bugger, whoever that was.

"That's... clever," Miles said. "How it happened, I have no idea. But I appreciate that you can tell when someone wrong is trying to use you for twisted ends."

Though it probably seemed odd to talk to his sword, the Borfblade quickly had become one of Miles's most reliable allies in his travels. A person can change their mind and switch sides, but Novasteel, it proved, cannot. Besides, a person who tends to travel and stand alone tends to talk to a lot of things that don't respond, because not responding is certainly easier to deal with than how people tend to do it.

Miles's breed of introversion aside, he now had to find and deal with Valras. Letting The Aura's Sight guide him again, he looked for the wayward Lysanarr. He couldn't have been too far, he had picked up the signature of both Valras and the Borfblade... in the same area.

"Oh..." Miles realized. "I mean... that's remarkably helpful. Good man. Eh, good sword?"

Miles recovered the Borfblade and left Valras's remains for pastures new, heading towards a cluster of rather volatile energy he was picking up.

As he approached the source, he started to figure out more what it was: An altar. The Siivalar were communing with a Demon, possibly even the Dark Six themselves, and that needed to be stopped. Another door between him and his quarry, and it was even the same guard from before, so Miles blasted both the guard and the door down with a potent wave of Psionic energy. There wasn't much left of either.

The Siivalar didn't seem to notice. They were entranced by the image they had conjured of what may become their new master. Fortunately, this allowed Miles to yank a few stones loose without interference, and the ritual went unstable, and inevitably fizzled out, ending with an audible snapping sound. The Siivalar in the room suddenly were confused, as if they didn't even know they had been in this room.

"The hell?" was just one of the many comments from the lot. Miles breathed a huge sigh of relief.

"Thank the gods I was in time," he then said. "Are you all aware of what has transpired here on Kalivan Tor?"

"Yes," one that was slightly more collected than the rest answered. "But we could do nothing. It was a waking nightmare, where our bodies moved beyond our will, and we spoke words that were not ours. Only us, however. Only us leaders."

"That means we have more problems, then," Miles noted. "In this time, your people were rather convinced of the Dark Six's legitimacy, especially since I would imagine that true name was never mentioned to them."

This was met by begrudging agreement.

"If you would be willing, helpful outsider, would you keep the true nature of what was going on with us a secret? The rest of the universe need not know precisely why we chose as we did."

"I see no harm in keeping your submission itself out of the picture. Duress only works for so long, I figure. If you wished, I would also be willing to stay on Kalivan Tor for some time and help rebuild, find a new way for the Siivalar Vulpians to be a part of the universe again."

Far more enthusiastic agreement followed, and Miles reached out to Revek on the neighboring world.

"Revek, can you hear me?" Miles asked.

"Oh, hell, I never get used to this," Revek replied aloud, wherever he was on Zharekk.

"I'd rather not be using this method, but I haven't

exactly got a more proper transmitter at the moment. Kalivan Tor is safe. Valras is dead, the Siivalar will be able to rebuild. You can call off that backup. I'll be sticking around for a bit to make sure everything goes right."

"Okay then," Revek acknowledged, and Miles stopped transmitting the telepathic message. Telepathic communication itself wasn't uncommon in the universe, let alone taboo, but it was seen as incredibly rude to forcibly enter someone's mind, regardless of whether or not they'd be able to tell. What Miles did would only be considered acceptable in its exact circumstance.

Miles sighed with relief once again. "All right, I've made sure no one will interfere, and that Kalivan Tor won't be getting any more visitors until it's ready."

Rebuilding Kalivan Tor needed to start at the very core of the planet. The machinery and tech was already there, it just needed to be repurposed to act as a Geothermal Power Generator instead of a Deoxian Pulse Engine. Such modifications were out of Miles's league, so he'd need to contact someone who knew about that sort of thing.

Miles used a transmitter he built from Valras's affects and what was left of his Defense Grid Generator, enough strength to access the general transmission frequencies of most of civilization. His contact of course, was on Laksor.

"Jaden?" Miles finally established the connection.

"Interesting setup," Jaden noted, given that Miles was using something that wasn't a traditional build for communications. "Revek tells me that you've made sure Kalivan Tor is safe from the Dark Six, but for some reason, he didn't have the Karma Scale."

"Long story. Do you know how one might repurpose a Deoxian Pulse Engine to just a Geothermal Power Generator? Planet-scale, core-level."

"The Deoxian Pulse Engine itself is just the ends to the mean. If there's a Deoxian Pulse Engine on the core, that means there's already a Geothermal Power Generator, and it's just tuned to making the Deoxian Pulse."

Miles also heard the scribbling of notes. Jaden was clearly writing down an epiphany.

"Regardless, the actual software that controls the generator would be reconfigurable to just generating and distributing electrical power across the planet, rather than powering up a Deoxian Pulse. Can you possibly send pictures of this thing? That would help."

The pictures weren't great, but it was the best he could do on such short notice, having to modify the transmitter like that. They certainly showed what needed be seen, and that was enough for Jaden to figure things out.

"Okay... this is actually pretty clever," Jaden said in an inquisitive tone. She was clearly thinking of a lot of things at once. "All right, that interface terminal would have the power distribution allocation means."

Miles walked over to the terminal, sifting through the menus and functions with Jaden's help. Soon, the engine was ready to distribute electrical power to any connected items.

"I mean... I don't particularly enjoy the idea of having all the cables lead to the core. Is there a way to project a sort of 'wireless power field' around the planet so that we very specifically do *not* have to worry about planet-level cable management?"

"Yeah, just set it to Pylon Mode."

"If only Tesla could see this," Miles said as he pressed the button, and the engine whirred to life, and Kalivan Tor's power was restored.

Once the planet had its power, and the Core-Fonts no longer needed charging, Miles could genuinely feel the collective sigh of relief of the planet and its peoples. Everything seemed to have worked out, even though Miles didn't feel like he had solidly *done* much in that moment. Perhaps it was because the switching of one power mode to another didn't have as much catharsis as flipping the lever to turn the whole setup on.

Though Miles wasn't getting the tingling feeling

of satisfaction, he wasn't going to lose sleep over it, if he were to sleep. Kalivan Tor had power again, and it could truly start to rebuild, now that just surviving didn't take the whole of the days.

Despite this, he couldn't shake the feeling that Kalivan Tor's trials weren't over yet. As much as he wanted to stay on the planet long enough for it all to work, Miles also wanted to see more of the universe. He had been intending to visit neighboring Raon-Arashal for a while now, and it kept getting put off in favor of... well, everything else. But Miles figured that his time to visit the home world of the Death World Vulpians would come soon enough.

"Raon-Arashal will come," Miles told himself. "Just... tomorrow, as it were."

"The Arena of Life," a voice said from behind him. None other than Tviri. Miles turned around to meet him.

"About that explaining, you can scratch that. I already understand," Miles responded as he pressed a few more buttons and got a little more familiar with the Geothermal Engine's systems. "I'm just glad I was able to stop it this time."

"This time?" Tviri asked, a hint of concern in his voice. Not for himself as much as Miles.

"A lot of my people fell to the Dark Six's temptations," Miles responded. "None of them are alive today, but I really don't care to know if they even bothered trying to atone."

"Why not?" Tviri's voice wasn't timid, but genuinely curious and wanting to learn.

"A shit planet of shit people is where I'm from," Miles affirmed. "I'm not even sure if I'm an exception. I don't think telling myself that I'm special is very convincing."

Tviri seemed to understand eventually, despite a few moments needed to mull it over.

"So... what now of the forward-stepped future?

Miles thought on that as Tviri approached the console. His words started, "I'm not entirely—" but were cut off as Tviri shoved Miles aside and pressed several buttons on the console, reactivating the protocol for the Deoxian Pulse.

"What in all the fucking realms?!" Miles yelled, switching over to The Aura's Sight for the first time since destroying the altar, only then realizing that he should've done it then. The Dark Six's connection never snapped. It never does. Miles's cursing and yelling as he charged a blast to destroy the core came too late, however.

A wave of energy, pulsing from the core of the engine pinned Miles against a nearby wall as it passed through the stone, and up throughout the planet, turning every Siivalar into servants of the Dark Six. Tviri had already ran off into the tunnels, and the Dark Six had Kalivan Tor in their yoke. But Miles was not Siivalar, and the Deoxian Pulse would not corrupt him, since it was not configured for his DNA. Likely the only time being human would save him. The wave retracted from the atmosphere, collapsing back into the core of the Deoxian Pulse Engine, and with a newfound fury, Miles slammed his hand into the ground, and with the power of The Aura, conjured a massive barrier around the planet, like he once did in Hulae to contain the Demons there.

"Now you're locked in here with me!" Miles seethed.

If his eyes could ripple with the rage of The Aura, they would have. Miles's anger knew no bounds today, the rage of Tviri's betrayal, the infuriation that he hadn't checked The Sight before, the hate of how much had to go wrong that just did, and only one goal among all that: Revenge. Not even vengeance, revenge for getting the better of him. Cutlass in left hand, pistol in right, he charged from the tunnel with intent to kill everything he saw, because all that was on this planet now was traitors.

The first guards he came across hadn't even fully been converted yet, they were still writhing with the Dark Six's grip wrestling their wills away, and putting them down with clean bullets to the head was just mercy. By the time Miles reached the first town, the

Siivalar people were gone, and so was his pity and his restraint. Cutting down dozens, gunning down hundreds more, and blasting away with The Aura, punching holes in their heads, chests and throats with bolts of Psionic energy. Every now and again, a wave shot across the ground to shatter the legs that were still on it, and cut the throats to stop the screaming. There was no mistake. Miles Radien had gone berserk in his retribution against the Siivalar, and he was now on the hunt for the one who pressed the accursed buttons: Tviri.

To Miles, this name meant deceiver now. Avanchenvaldr on Earth was *a* deceiver, but Tviri was now the word that was the phenomenon of lies itself to him. Traitors require prior loyalty, but whatever Demon had control of who he thought was his friend had been planning this all along, likely since the Aura Runner first landed on this forsaken planet.

The Siivalar did attack Miles on sight, but with fledgling power, as the vessels of the Demon's wills were only still adjusting to being the conduits of Hell, and their strikes, handily countered. Their lives, quickly extinguished. Their souls, quickly released from the tormenting servitude they had entered willingly.

This was what enraged Miles the most. They agreed to it. They chose to serve the Demons. These people, who despite all knowledge and all history for them to study and know that the Dark Six were the enemy, did still willingly choose to think that they would be the exceptions to the rule. But that's what they all think. It's what all the humans on Earth that served them thought.

Human or Siivalar, it made no difference now. To Miles, the Siivalar were no longer Vulpians in his eyes. Not since the instant that Deoxian Pulse ravaged the will of the planet and its populace, that he now stood to exterminate. Not a thought towards whatever aftermath, whatever repercussion, it didn't matter in these moments. All that needed to be known was that Kalivan Tor just became a planet of traitors. And even on Earth, Miles never handled betrayal lightly, let alone gracefully.

He could sense how many were left, just like on Hulae, when his friend there had a counter, whose name escaped him. It wasn't the priority. The priority was once again to make the number of Demonic presences zero.

Cities, depopulated. Villages and boroughs, now as empty as they had appeared when he first arrived. Even after the initial bloodbath, Miles's intent and ferocity remained the same, even if not his brutality. That brutality became cold, focused precision, and the ruin of Kalivan Tor's people. The Siivalar themselves had destroyed the remaining scattered species not taken by

<FIRE TO BURN THE STARS>

the Deoxian Pulse, and all that was left was them, and Miles. Something he intended to change.

Days passed, as this one-man crusade continued. Days became weeks and months, but Miles felt no acknowledgment of time's passage as more and more of his newfound enemies fell at the tip of his sword. The AZP-621 pistol had run dry long ago, and what munitions he had scavenged were also spent, save for one bullet. Every kill was just that more personal now, and Miles had his revenge, over and over again. The numbers dwindled, and then there was one: The only one who was running this whole time. None other than the liar Tviri, and Miles had him cornered.

"You know—" Tviri started, but Miles fired one last shot from his pistol to end that sentence.

"You lost the right to last words when you chose betrayal," Miles spat.

And then there were none.

All life on Kalivan Tor was only Miles Radien.

Only then did he stop.

Only then did he take a deep breath. Only then did he think. And the first thing he did was to return to the Torgaen Fields, and the fog being who told him he had a chance to save the Siivalar.

"You said that it wasn't set," Miles sternly spoke. "You said I had a chance."

‹GREGOR FJELLREV›

"What would you have done if I hadn't?" the spirit lamented. "We both had impossible choices to make."

Words just couldn't happen. He had none. As much as he more than had the strength in his arms to sheath his sword, he couldn't bring himself to do anything but let its edge grind against the sandstone floor as he made his way back to that first grand city, and slumped against the same pillar he once had done with wonderment.

The slump became a seat, and the clang of the Borfblade hitting the ground echoed through the cold, dark halls. Cold only in atmosphere, the planet was still close to its star, and The Aura still was needed to keep Miles's skin from catching on fire.

"No victory today," Miles finally spoke heavily. "No honor, no win... nothing."

He just sat there, gods only know how long for. Every breath was another heavy sigh.

"I was too young to feel world-weary on Earth," he continued to himself. "I still am."

He looked up and saw a familiar Effigy sitting across from him, like it was ready once again to listen.

"Why are you still here?" Miles questioned. "You should abandon me, I failed! I failed what I should stand for! What you *would* stand for! You never would have committed genocide! You would have found a way! Find someone worth saving, someone worth listening to, it's not me!"

There were no tears in Miles's eyes, they had all been spent long ago. But the weight remained, and there was no mistake of that.

"I came here to save a species, and fetch an artifact, and what I've done couldn't be further from it if I tried! You have no reason to be within a galaxy of me! It's more than your right to abandon me! Hell, I advise you do!"

A moment passed. Nothing changed.

"I committed genocide here. How the hell do you even come back from that? You can't. It doesn't happen. Does it even matter if it was justified in the sick way that it would be here? I know the Siivalar had already died, I know that. The Demons in the husks were what I cut down. But even then, a species died because I couldn't save them..."

"How could I have, though? Who would have done this, if not me?"

"I just don't get it. I don't get any of it."

Hours later, Miles remembered he still had the transmitter he had used to contact Jaden, and he tuned it to a familiar contact on Zharekk.

"Moldrenor, it's Radien. My ship still on that planet?"

"Yup, Revek left it here after he found his own way back to Laksor."

Miles's voice was heavy, and Moldrenor could tell. But Moldrenor didn't say anything, Miles was in his darkest hour, and the last thing he needed was for someone to condescendingly say 'didn't go well?'

"All right, good." Miles said, switching off the transmitter and calling to the Aura Runner to get to the surface of the planet.

Miles just continued to sit, leaning against that pillar, that was quite honestly proving a more consistent friend than anyone who had lived on this planet of traitors. Even when his ship pinged him Psionically to let him know it had arrived, Miles still sat there for a while longer.

"Radien stands alone," he reminded himself before he stood up and retraced his route to the planet's surface. "The oldest truth." Once he got to his ship, the first order of business was to inform Cynofrax of what the hell just happened.

On his arrival home, Arakai was at the platform. Apparently, he had forgotten that Miles was heading to Kalivan Tor, and had planned to visit.

"Hey, Arakai," Miles greeted.

"You don't seem well." Arakai noted.

"I'm fuckin' pissed, that's what. I need to debrief

Cynofrax on what the hell just happened"

It wasn't long before Miles had his audience with Cynofrax's Conclave, and recounted the betrayal on Kalivan Tor.

"The Siivalar of Kalivan Tor betrayed me. Betrayed everything. Betrayed the whole damn universe in pursuit of getting to say that they had the power. I was showing them a better way. I was making it work, and with time, they'd arrive at that point. But no, they wanted it now, like a bunch of whiny children. As much as I understand why their impatience existed, it's no excuse. There *is* no excuse for this. They knew, they knew I was giving them what they wanted, but they gave their whole fucking selves to the Dark Six anyway! The whole species, the whole-ass species swore allegiance to *them!*" he finished.

Several of the leaders of Cynofrax were surprised at this, but their own power told them that Miles was not lying. Everything he was telling them was fact, this account really is what took place on Kalivan Tor.

"Such brazen treason is inexcusable for any that would call themselves Vulpian!" Miles continued, to the response of nods from at least two of the Conclave. "The traitor caste, the Siivalar proved themselves, and I cannot call them Vulpian! No, I would exile them from the ranks of the species! I would name them the traitors they are, and the whole fucking planet as well! The Planet of

Traitors, that's what I'd call Kalivan fucking Tor now!"

A quick moment passed before Miles finished his testimony.

"I would expect this from Humans, not Vulpians!"

Miles soon after excused himself from the Conclave hall, leaving the remaining action in their hands. Miles wanted to make no more decisions about that planet, or anyone that once lived on it. Arriving at his home, he poured himself a generous amount of Kalisaine's Root, the gin-like spirit he had grown fond of during his time on Cynofrax. A gimlet made of this stuff was certainly a force to be reckoned with.

A knock on his door. It was Veralis.

"You don't need to be here," Miles informed.

"I know I don't *need* to," was her response.

"Then you are free to go, and you know it. I will deal with this myself, and you do not need to burden yourself with my troubles."

"The hell makes you say that? A whole planet succumbed to the Dark Six, and you had an impossible choice! How can you choose to face that on your own?!"

"Because it is my burden, Veralis!" It wasn't a shout, but Miles certainly made clear his stance on the matter. "I was the one who had that choice to make, I was the one who chose, carried it out, therefore *I* am the one who must live with it! *I* am the one who must carry that weight until the end of my days! No one should weigh themselves with the troubles that are mine! It is not my place to impose that you must help, it is not my place to throw this onto someone else's shoulders, because it is *my* burden! It's not supposed to become yours as well!"

Miles just sat there, and then downed the rest of his drink. He didn't bother getting up to grab another. Didn't want to numb this pain, because he had earned it.

"Action and reaction, choice and consequence. I understand that my choice was impossible, I understand that very likely, others would have done the same. But at the end of the day, it was me that did it."

Veralis just stood there, and sighed, but not with disappointment or exasperation. Though it was sure what that sigh wasn't, it wasn't entirely sure what it was.

"Radien... that really is what you'd say. It means that at the very least, if nothing else, you're still Radien. Uncompromisingly, unwaveringly Radien. Take that as a compliment."

Miles didn't even look up as Veralis sat down next to him.

"There is no surprise in how you see it from me. Radien would say, feel and think those things for sure. You're so far from Earth now, and I know more than most that old understandings die hard. So in this moment, understand you're talking to me and no human, knowing that you're on Cynofrax and not Earth... what do you need?"

Miles didn't say anything. He just leaned into her, hesitantly resting his head on her arm, and Veralis let him. It was a start.

GLOSSARY OF PLANETS
PLUS ADDITIONAL
INFORMATION AND TRIVIA

Cynofrax – Capitol world and origin planet of the Vulpians and their predecessor race, the Old Cynofraxians, this planet stands as one of the most vital for the preservation of a generally united universe free of Demonic presence. The Aura Prism, atop Cynofrax's single mountain (There is a mountain range on Cynofrax, but none of those individual mountains have names, given that it's a mountainous collective) known as The Mountain, holds strong the barriers between mortal reality and the Burning Hells, domain of the Dark Six (Though the Dark Six themselves do not actually reside within the Burning Hells,

<FIRE TO BURN THE STARS>

instead a prison dimension known as *Unapasakl Aura-Käynenrel,* roughly translating as "Eternally power-destroying place," or more colloquially, "Doomrealm"). Though not absolute and invulnerable to Demonic incursion, the alternate would be having no such barriers. Cynofrax is also one of only two known planets to have a Sub-Ocean, an exceedingly rare phenomenon in which beneath the floor of the planetary ocean, there exists a second ocean beneath that before the ocean crust and subsequent mantle of the planet. The Cynofraxian Sub-Ocean has not been explored in any amount, let alone charted, though it is the case that Cynofrax's planetary ocean itself does have civilization presences in calmer areas of the surface and beneath.

Kalivan Tor – The closest to its parent star in the Strife Planets Celestial Array, Kalivan Tor's few societies live entirely underground, one of few to successfully do so. The most common of these societies are of the Siivalar Vulpian species, though scattered others live within the subterranean cities and tunnels that make up the living presence on this old world. It is theorized that Kalivan Tor, however, was not always in such a state of thermal battering from its parent star.

Surface expeditions conducted in the past have shown that at some point, the planet was in fact, within the habitable zone of its star. It is not known whether or not Kalivan Tor was pushed into closer orbit by an external source, or if the star expanded, which would be highly atypical of its type. Regardless, the Siivalar were able to adapt to the surface's hostility and move entirely underground, garnering the necessary resources for survival both from the underground, and possibly from massive surface emergency stores from before the event at first.

Fortem Terra Nova – With the Human species's involvement with the Conclave of Sentience, among the first things granted to the fledgling peoples was an uncolonized planet fit for such, that the first steps towards proper expansion into being a spacefaring race could begin. As is often the case with a species's second world after their origin planet, every founded city thus far has been named "New (name of major city on origin planet)" Though the Conclave of Sentience remains suspicious of the Humans overall, given both their past and the special conditions that had to be set forth for their inclusion, it is far from denied that there are promising subjects within, and that the Humans have the potential to make great technological and psionic contributions to the universe at large, some even postulating that the Humans could become 'The next Eluria.'

Turazin – Formerly known as Kendrossos V, Turazin is under normal circumstances, home to only two structures: The Hideout and the Spire of the Conclave, wherein the Conclave of Sentience convenes within its underground level, since the Spire itself mostly acts as a physical landmark to signify where the actual meeting place of the Conclave is, and unlike what traditional knowledge and convention might suggest, the top level is not the chambers of the Conclave, it is an observatory. Of course, since no law states that there must *only* be two structures on Turazin, the Humans did construct a research facility on the planet, not far from The Hideout. It is not entirely understood precisely why The Hideout is called such, especially since it is a rather ornate structure upon its outside. However, it has been theorized that this might be a sort of 'cosmic Anglicization' of sorts towards its name in the Kendrosian language, *Hithosson,* meaning 'library' in Ethi Kendrosian, the main dialectic form on the planet. This has not been confirmed, especially considering that Kendrossos V/Turazin was, and still is the least populated planet of the Kendrosium System.

Korvideyl – The crystal planet of Korvideyl has been a source of scientific intrigue ever since its discovery in the Fourth Cosmic Era. The entire planet is lined with caverns containing crystals of varying effect, some benevolent, others mischievous, and others deadly. There have been categorized no less than five thousand different crystal forms in Korvideyl's caves, all of varying effect with varying degrees of utility. One of the more famous uses of Korvideyl's crystals was in the creation of the Honorblade of Korvideyl, which used what was described as an 'Honor Stone' from the planet. The Honorblade of Korvideyl renders its wielder completely invulnerable to being attacked from behind, or at range. The only way to defeat someone wielding the Honorblade of Korvideyl is to do so face to face, in honorable combat. Korvideyl Station, constructed on the planet's single moon, has graduated from simply being dedicated to studying the crystal planet to a major scientific hub in general since its construction.

!leysa - !leysa is the home planet of the avian Corvuseine species. They are a rather enigmatic species compared to other Conclave races, given their relatively uncommon nature. Though not endangered by any means, the Corvuseine simply manage to 'happen to keep to themselves,' as it were. !leysa is also a hotspot for the development of improved agricultural technologies, making the world a hidden gem of sorts, particularly when compared to nearby Teyn-Var-Wolk. As a result of its heightened priority on agriculture, !leysa is also home of some of the most prestigious culinary schools in the known universe, as well as a thriving population of novelists and storywriters that often specialize in Morality Plays.

Homphalion – A planet lined with mountain ranges and tall plateaus, Homphalion certainly has an aesthetic highly appealing to the types of people that like the idea of living in small towns in the mountains. Even the plateau cities manage to achieve this sort of style despite being entire cities. Homphalion's distance from its parent star puts the planet in a constant winter, which eventually gave birth to the planet's main cultural draw: The Alpine Combat League. This is an orbital-year-long open snowball fighting tournament across the planet which almost the

<GREGOR FJELLREV>

entire population partakes within, and each individual has their own score and ranking within the Alpine Combat League. At the end of the year, the top one thousand scorers in each division compete in a massive free-for-all battle in Homphalion's City of Arenas, until only one remains to claim the title of Alpine Combat Champion for that year.

Trylaxia – Trylaxia is a completely inhospitable planet whose native flora and fauna are so deadly and nightmarish, it almost seems comical. Some neighboring planets, in their early theologies, called Trylaxia "the refuse heap to host the gods' failed experiments," since creatures such as the Skyspiders, known to swarm in numbers in the thousands with venom described as "liquid suffering," and the Rageflower, which upon blooming releases a toxic cloud capable of dissolving any organic matter within a radius of several meters make Trylaxia the butt of many jokes about staggeringly hostile environments. The Trylaxian species is actually homed on the planet's two moons, and it is believed that life was able to propagate on those moons due to the introduction of Firetree Spores laced with amino acids that had been launched into space due to

<FIRE TO BURN THE STARS>

the explosive nature of the deaths of Trylaxian Firetrees.

Teyn-Var-Wolk – Teyn-Var-Wolk is the home world of both the Woran Cos and Nuvenr Draconian species, two races with exceptional Psionic tendencies, well above the average latent power present in all sentient life. As such, Teyn-Var-Wolk's cities and civilizations favor the use of Psionic technologies over traditional mechanical technologies, akin to Cynofrax. The planet's Artificer schools demonstrate also the creativity of Teyn-Var-Wolk's peoples, having created such artifacts as the Cey-Tavn Shroud, and the Ring of the Narrator, among others with intriguingly specific abilities and effects.

Caren'Das – Capitol world of the Hajivakk, Caren'Das is a major trade hub for the connected universe, given how much space the planet has, being decently larger than typical solid-rock planets, and having six moons of respectable size as well. The Exemplar of the Haji-Son typically lives on Caren'Das, but this is not absolute. Being such a central and key planet, Caren'Das has both its fortunate and unfavorable traits. For example, it is actually recommended that one does not attempt to raise a family on Caren'Das. While the

<GREGOR FJELLREV>

massive amount of trade might seem to present an equally massive amount of opportunity and flexible paths of career, this actually works in the opposite manner. The sheer scale of trade and population makes it extremely difficult to find any work, with such a huge body of competition, often fierce and far more experienced than anyone trying to start making a name for themselves. It is also the case that because there are so many people on Caren'Das, those seeking to employ can afford to be extremely selective and picky of who they hire, since there's that many fish in the sea, as it were. Consequently, Caren'Das is a good place to visit, and live so long as you don't intend to start a family. At least, one that won't grow bitter in their adulthood for the vicious lack of chances to prove themselves.

Mjarfus – Mjarfus is the Origin Planet of the Hajivakk, but actually isn't too terribly populated these days. This is mostly due to the planet's relative tectonic instability compared to the other worlds in the Nashira Strand solar system, and the resultant commonality of natural disasters. However, cities on Mjarfus have consistently improved their durability during such disasters, to the point that some entire regions are considered hurricane-proof as long as people stay indoors when it happens. Most cities on Mjarfus have flood channels beneath their sidewalks, and transit stations often have a dedicated 'lane' for flood water. Mjarfus is considered an excellent place to live if you like to live in simple day-to-day manner, not focusing on much other than making sure you've got enough to get to the next one.

Killentarn – Killentarn serves as both the Capitol World of the Varok-Torividan, and is a major center of culture between the reptilian species and the mechanical Ascendant. During the Sentience War, Killentarn was the hub of resistance against the fascist slaver species known as the Shard, both for the Ascendant and for Varok-Torividan groups fed up with the complacency of their representative government on the former Capitol World of Terevetz. Killentarn is considered one of the fastest progressing planets on the front of social ideologies, and the current standard for which new sentient species are recognized, The Pillars Three, was ratified on this planet. As of late, however, there has been a relative silence from Killentarn and its people, as very few ships have been leaving the planet since the early Eighth Cosmic Era, relative to the amount of traffic to

<GREGOR FJELLREV>

and from the planet during Killentarn's golden age of ideological progress.

Raon-Arashal – Home of the Death World Vulpians, Raon-Arashal translates as "The Arena of Life" from Old Cynofraxian. This title is meant as "the arena that is life" and not "the arena where life happens," which fortunately avoids the pretentious artistic metaphor of a flower blooming from the ashes and blood of an arena. This suits the Death Worlders nicely, since they are not known for their fondness or patience of pretentious artistic metaphors, being a very practical species of Vulpians. Death World Vulpians, though not uncommon, are the least numerous Vulpian type among the recognized variations, of which there are ten nine: The three major variants, descended from the Old Cynofraxians (Cynofrax, Talvas, Death World) and the seven six descendants of those major variants. From the Cynofrax Vulpians, there descended the Crimsonian, Bendorkin and Lørkas Vulpians, from the Talvas Vulpians, the Noregenas and Dor-Val-Der Vulpians, and from the Death Worlders, the Zharekai and Siivalar.

———————

CHARACTER AND LOCATION

TRIVIA

♦ Veralis Stratenheim's twin axes are named Käyner and Käynvi. Translated from the Old Cynofraxian language, this means "Doom number one" and "Doom number two."

♦ Arakai Selendica, despite his fascination with longrifles, the more bells and whistles the better, is actually not a great marksman, having focused more on his swordsmanship. Speaking of swords, the two that Arakai wields have an extra flair to them where they set any wounds they cause on fire. Though Arakai claims this is mostly for the purpose of more effectively 'stunning' his enemies with his hits and the intimidation factor, it is also the case that he thought it would be really cool to have swords that set the wounds they make on fire.

♦ Micah Jorvask despises the idea of poisoning weapons, and becomes greatly perturbed when people ask if the parrying dagger she keeps in her off-hand while in combat is poisoned. She is also a 'security tester' by hobby, by which she, at the request of a given proprietor, breaks into facilities and attempts to steal items for the purpose of testing how well they are guarded.

♦ Jarrek Wöllschlager, Arch-Militant of the Redarian Interplanetary Battlefleet (the space branch of the Velani Militarium) is reputed for faking his death when he needs to take some time off for vacation, since he would rather not be a bother by asking for it, even though as such a valuable person to the Militarium, it would be given to him willingly. As of late, it has become a sort of running gag, and Jarrek does not put much effort into the actual story of how he died this time, as it were. In fact, the most recent one was preceded by him approaching a senior staff, declaring "I'm gonna go die for a bit, I'll let you know when I survive," then flopping on the ground and rolling out of the room, halfheartedly despairing of his imminent demise.

♦ Micah Jorvask is actually one of the leading authorities on the study of Keystone Gems, and was considered to make the announcement of the discovery of the Korvideyl Optima Geode. However, she insisted that Kor-Vas-Tarn make the announcement, since he was the one who actually found the gem itself.

\<GREGOR FJELLREV\>

♦ Xenidar Ralkas has been known to, when bored, utilize a Personal Gravity Polarity Manipulator to allow himself to 'loaf' on the walls and ceiling of The Hideout, and watch the confused reactions of visitors and patrons when they see a Talvas Vulpian casually ignoring traditional gravity.

♦ Jaden of Laksor once stabbed a Human for suggesting that the GAMA should be made to be be capable of turning non-humans into Humans. It is unknown whether or not that Human died from the wound or was forcibly turned into a Laksorian. However, the Human was not missed either way, given his reputation for attempting to swindle locals. When asked about the ultimate fate of this Human, Jaden's response was simply "Mess with rabbit, you get the stabbit."

♦ The Hykentiu Dorg's favorite tactic in fighting is to constantly use throws on his opponents, to both wear them out and frustrate them into expending more energy in their tension. It often takes Miirkae finishing such opponents off to get Dorg to move on to the next one already.

♦ Planetary Guardsmen act as law enforcement in metropolitan areas of civilized worlds, and are explicitly forbidden from carrying offensive weapons. They are granted a shield, and their armor is made of a lightweight polymer capable of rendering benign most forms of projectile and melee weaponry. Coupled with extensive training and their shields, they have zero need to carry weapons, and to even so much as sharpen the edges of their shield is nearly a capital offense, which carries the mandatory penalty of immediate and permanent dismissal from duty, as well as prohibition from serving in any Planetary Guard in the future, a hefty monetary fine and prison sentence. Some planets also permit RHS (Ritual Honorable Suicide) for Guardsmen that violate their duty as a last symbol of honor reclamation, as such disgrace more often than not permanently destroys the livelihood of violators. Individuals who have served within a planet's military are not permitted to serve as Guardsmen. Rural areas have slightly more leniency, especially when wild animal attacks are a real and potential threat. However, such places hardly ever employ Planetary Guardsmen, instead opting for a collective protection model in which citizens within the area are all trained in basic marksmanship and swordsmanship, and weapons may not be loaded when in the towns themselves.

♦ The Lysanarr homeworld of Gelvetori is a hub for craft spirits in the universe, and accolades from yearly libation

<GREGOR FJELLREV>

competitions are considered among the most prestigious a distillery can attain.

♦ Demon hunting organizations, such as the Chorgon Nehr and the Order of ETK have rocky relations with city-based 'traditional' law enforcement agencies, in no small part because the Demon Hunters are often far better at keeping order during crisis than the actual authorities. In fact, it is now believed that the backlash against the Chorgon Nehr on Gliropa was due to a smear campaign from the police of the city of Oothaj, after a Demonic incursion failed spectacularly thanks to the aid of the Chorgon Nehr, while Oothaj police were utterly inept and useless during the incursion, to the point of deliberate negligence. Unfortunately, the propaganda was well-received by the public on Gliropa, which arguably paved the way for the nearly successful incursion in Hulae. The footage often touted as proof of the Chorgon Nehr's incompetency, as it turned out, was from one of its member's military career prior to joining the Chorgon Nehr, and the actual friendly fire incident was not perpetuated by the member himself.

♦ The Old Cynofraxian word *Aurhaldt* is the word for "to converse." It is also the word for "to imprison."